BEN STI

GW00374723

ME, YOU, CHARLEY

AND MUM

TRIPLEe PUBLICATIONS

TRIPLEe BOOKS

SENIBONG COVE, MALAYSIA

81750

FIRST PUBLISHED AUGUST 2020

PRINTED & PUBLISHED BY AMAZON KDP in association

WITH TRIPLEe PUBLICATIONS

ISBN 9798638286705

EDITED by VALERIE HART

ME, YOU, CHARLEY AND MUM

ONE

"And do you Henry James Cahill take Kelly Joyce Carter to be your lawful wedded wife?" I was listening to the vicar but also looking behind my soon to be wife and seeing her sister, who was also her chief bridesmaid, stood less than a foot behind her and at her mum in the front row, who was just glaring at me, and all I was thinking was; *What the fuck am I marrying into?!*

Fourteen months earlier.

"Can you get me to Swallow in five minutes?" Said this woman getting into the back of my cab rather hurriedly.

"I beg your pardon?" I replied.

"Swallow Avenue? I need to be there for 10am. It's 9.55, no, 9.56 now. Can you hurry!?"

"I'll give it a go" I said driving off, smirking to myself.

We arrived at one minute past so not too bad. The attractive dark-haired lady, with the huge sunglasses, paid and off she went. My name is Harry, well, it's officially Henry. Why Harry is a version of Henry I do not know. It's the same number of letters so it's not to make the name shorter, like a Mike from a Michael. In fact Henry could be shortened to Hen I suppose, so Harry could even be a longer version of what was necessary. But none the less I'd always been known as Harry. I wonder why I was called Henry at birth but all my family called me Harry? Anyway, that's not important really. I bet Prince Harry is a Henry. But, I digress.

I drive a taxi in and around Bromley, trying my best to avoid central London whenever possible. I actually quite like the job. I was brought up by my Uncle and when he died a few years back I was left his house and some money. This job covers my lifestyle, which is pretty mundane really but having no mortgage and a biggish house on the outskirts of London meant I was in a pretty sound position. *'You lucky twat'* my mate said to me not long after my Uncle's death. Not *quite* how I saw it.

Mind you, my friend in question we called Rocket. Probably because Trigger had been taken by Only Fools and Horses and the fact we knew a Bullet earlier in our lives. Poor Bullet was arrested after a botched armed robbery. I say armed robbery but only the bloke he did the robbery with actually had a gun, on the day that they robbed the bookies, Bullet couldn't find his gun so took his girlfriend's rampant rabbit vibrator and tried to pass it off as a gun. At least it was black. To be fair the staff were so preoccupied with the bloke that had the sawn-off shotgun that they didn't really pay attention to poor Bullet and the fact *he* was the only other actual weapon in the shop. They were caught because the next day Bullet went back to the same bookies to put a bet on with the recently stolen money and asked the woman behind the counter if she recognised him from yesterday, forgetting he was in robbing the place. They were sentenced to 15 years. So now we have Rocket, because everyone has one in their group right?

Anyway, after I dropped Ms Swallow I was driving out of the street and I saw a car with its bonnet up. I'm a decent bloke; don't know much about cars but I do know a lot about nice legs. It was these said legs that made my mind up to pull over and offer help. (I'd have stopped anyway honestly.) I swung around at the end of the street and pulled up in front.

I got out of the car and headed over to the woman with her head buried in the engine. As I got ready to ask if she wanted some help I suddenly became very paranoid about what I was wearing. We'd been given these cheap polo shirts to wear by the owner of the firm but he only bought them in extra-extra-large. I'd imagine it was because it was a cheap job-lot but I guess it also made sense as most drivers on the firm would need at least an extra-large. I however did not. It swamped me. I'm tall but not wide and tended to tuck the shirt in on one side to try and get some sort of definition but the shoulders were the killer, the arm seams were pretty much at my elbows. I looked like a small boy that had been given a full grown man's top. Even though I was a fully grown man. Still too late now, plus also what are the odds on this woman caring? Her car was knackered and she was probably in a foul mood. And let's be honest, if she's hot she's not going to be interested in taxi driver that looks like he only shops at Jacamo.

"Hi, everything okay?" Stupid start. Obviously it isn't.

She turned around and smiled. She was a cracker! Obviously I became an instant stuttering mess.

"Scrap that, I meant can I help I should have said, asked, I see not everything isn't, I mean is, okay" I said. The word scrap came with a big bit of spit flying out. This is just going *great*.

"Oh thank you," she said after politely following my blob of spit to the ground. "I'm not sure what's happened, it just started to lose power so I pulled over. Do you know much about cars?"

"Only how to drive them" I said sounding like some sort of exciting getaway driver not a bored nearly part-time cabbie. "Let's have a look though"

She moved aside and I leant in. She smelt lovely and I was pleased she stayed close and looked under the bonnet the same time as me. What the fuck I was looking for or at I had no idea. Let's crack out a couple of mmm's and arrrhs to at least give the impression I know a little. I'll even give something a shake maybe. NOT THAT! Whatever it was I touched, it was boiling! It made me pull my arm away in a hurry and I elbowed her right in the tit.

"Jesus, shit. Ouch!" She said, obviously, and pulled away grabbing her bashed boob.

"Fuck! Shit, so sorry" I said as reaching out to grab the aggrieved nork. Luckily I stopped myself before grabbing it. Didn't really need a sexual harassment charge today.

"What the hell?!" She said. I was mortified. (But also kind of enjoying watching the attractive lady rub herself in front of me!) My god I'm such a fucking loser.

"I'm so so sorry. Shit. Are you okay?"

"Well I'm at lot worse than I was 20 seconds ago!"

"I'm so embarrassed. My god! Sorry." And this was followed by probably the most awkward silence of my life. It was probably only ten or twenty seconds but felt about a month. "At least they're big enough to take a hit"

OH MY GOD. What is wrong with me?!

She stopped rubbing and just looked at me. I was waiting for her to tell me to basically just fuck off.

"That is probably the weirdest thing anyone has ever said to me."

"I can honestly say I have absolutely no idea why I said it either," I responded in a strange wobbling way holding my hands out in apology and maybe ready to block a punch.

Nothing came.

"Look" I started "I'm sorry about your car, I don't know what the problem is and I'm doubly sorry about your, erm, thing there. I really am. Can I give you a lift anywhere or maybe tow you to a garage or something?" I wasn't expecting her to want to get in a car with me after this.

"Well I need to catch a train so maybe you could run me to the station? I need to get to a meeting"

"No problem, brilliant. Thank you, yes no problem at all."

"Great. Let me just grab my bag and lock the car up. It'll be okay here for the day wont it?"

"Yeah I don't see why not, no yellow lines or anything. Plus I'll be working today so will check on it when I'm near." I said this thinking it was a bizarre thing to say. It's a car. It's locked. It's in a residential street. But as bizarre things by me go today, this was nothing.

She got her jacket and bag from the front seat and I put down the bonnet. She pressed the fob to lock it and started walking towards my car. She really was a good looking woman I thought as I gestured with my arm for her walk in front of me as she swung her suit type jacket on. I followed with the intention of getting along side of her and then opening the door for her. I quickly looked back at her car to make sure all was okay and obviously didn't see her stop right in front of me. She'd apparently stopped to check her bag for house keys. This can't be done whilst walking it seemed. I walked right into the back of her with a thud, pushing her and me, on top of her, from behind, onto my car's bonnet. Jesus Christ.

"Shit, sorry!" I said pressing myself up off her and the bonnet.

Luckily she got herself back upright and was laughing. Laughing and pushing her hair back out of her face. I'm glad she was laughing and not thinking this was a full on sex attack.

I started laughing too.

"I didn't see that you had stopped"

"Its fine" she said still laughing "totally my fault, I shouldn't have stopped dead in front of you"

"I should have been looking where I was going; I was just checking your car"

"Don't worry about it." She said straightening herself out a bit and starting walking towards the passenger side of my car. "Anyway, my *ample*-sized boobs broke the fall!"

I liked her. I smiled and headed round to get into the driver's seat.

"I'm Kelly by the way," she said across the roof. A safe distance from me I thought.

"Nice to meet you Kelly. I'm Harry."

"Nice shirt Harry." She smiled and got into the car.

TWO

That was how we first met, a simple twist of fate. I dropped her at the station that morning but arranged to pick her up again when she came back on the train that afternoon. It was the least I could have done. After all, I'd spent the morning accidentally touching her up. I got her from the station around 2pm. On the journey back to her car, which apparently been fixed during the day, she was obviously very efficient; I made my move and asked her out. It was a bold move given how we started but the journey in the morning made me think she would be open to an evening out. She made it clear she didn't have a boyfriend or husband. Or girlfriend or wife I suppose. We also had texted each other a couple of times in the day (her first) and it was quite flirtatious, I always found it easier to have a flirt on the text, I would be a mess if I had to actually say some things to an *actual* woman. Not that there was anything dirty, she certainly didn't seem that type, but it was definitely a free flowing conversation. Even if it was only by text. I was hoping it would flow freely in person as well, even if it would probably be a slightly more awkward version.

We decided to go out on the Thursday evening. It was the middle of June so it was quite pleasant out and about. The wine flowed and so did the conversation, thankfully. She was a real laugh. We'd done a bottle and a half of wine by now and it was starting to show a little in our giddiness.

"So," she started "I was in this really fancy Italian place with my ex, sorry to mention him but it's a good story"

"Carry on, I'm sure someone as pretty as you has a lot of ex's." Now that was supposed to sound much more like a compliment than it did.

"Erm, I'm not sure how to take that?!"

I didn't think she was ready for me to back it up with another joke about how she takes it.

"Yeah, sorry, I say sorry a lot to you don't I? I didn't mean it to sound like you put it about. Quite the opposite in fact. You could be very picky?!" Shut up you twat. Shut up now.

"Okaaaay." At least she was smiling.

"Carry on, please. Let's laugh at your ex, which isn't one of many. But doesn't matter if it is. We've all been there making mistakes" SHUT THE FUCK UP! What was I even going on about?

Luckily, or probably thanks to the wine, she just burst out laughing. "You are *really* shit at this aren't you?!"

"Only when I really like who I'm with" Smooth I thought. "Honestly, I'm like James Bond when I'm with a right dog."

This made her laugh more and I topped up our glasses.

"Anyway, as I was saying."

"This had better be good now."

"Shut up, it is. I was in a restaurant and he had ordered pizza, a seafood one which should have sparked alarm bells anyway, but when the waiter brings it over he moans that it's not sliced. He was obviously only ever used to Dominoes. So the waiter picks it up and goes to take it to the kitchen. Before he takes it he asks Richard, his name by the way, if he wants it cut into six or into eight. Richard thinks for a second before saying; *just six please, I'll never eat eight.* How funny is that?"

"That is pretty funny." I replied smiling away. "I've got a mate just like that!"

"And I bet he's worth having about just to keep you entertained? Tell me one."

"I'll tell you a couple." I said as she finished off the bottle into our glasses.

"We call him Rocket. A few years ago his dad sent him to the shop to get some cigarettes; he was probably about nineteen-twentyish at the time and still lived at home. *Okay dad, which ones?* 'Get me twenty Embassy lad' his dad told him. *What if they haven't got them?* 'Then just get me anything'. And off he went. Turned out they didn't have any Embassy. So instead, do you know what he took his dad back? A pork pie"

"Oh my."

"Yep, his dad just shook his head and asked what was wrong with him. 'How can I smoke a frigging pork pie?!' He did eat it though. Another time we were in Spain on a lad's holiday and he said it was like living in a foreign country for two-weeks."

Kelly was just giggling into her wine by this point.

"We tried telling him that it was a foreign country but all he kept saying was *but not when you're in it it's not. As Spanish people don't call it foreign.*"

We carried on laughing and talking through another bottle of wine. Work early in the morning was already down the pan. It was approaching the awkward part of the evening where you have to decide what's going to happen. When I say decide, I mean SHE will decide what's going to happen. Turned out we had a bit of a kiss over the table, I gentle kiss with a little sneak of a tongue. And when I was putting her coat on her we had a proper one. But then she made it clear that that was that tonight, separate taxis, and asked if we fancied meeting up Saturday. Obviously I did and was also glad that she wasn't putting out. I don't think I was happy at the time about that but it said a lot about her. Hopefully.

As we were waiting for her cab to arrive, we had another little kiss and held each other in the slightly summer-chilled air. As what we thought her cab was pulling up we moved forward. It was hers but first out jumped six Asian women, one of them with an L-plate on.

"Watch out, Hen-do." I said to her.

"No" she briskly said back. "Hindu."

She got in the taxi, both of us drunk laughing at her funny joke and off she went. I watched the car as it disappeared down the road. I was already looking forward to Saturday. Even if she might be mildly racist.

Three

The Saturday soon came round and I met her at the station early afternoon. I planned to take her into the city for some food and lots of booze! We got to Covent Garden around 3pm and I took her straight to my favourite food place in the world. *Pie's from the Skye's* was a little pie shop that did the nicest food. Every time I came to the city I'd go here. Obviously I didn't eat pies every week, otherwise I'd soon be filling my work shirt, but I knew the staff, so I must come more than I should. It was as busy as ever but we were soon served.

"Hi Harry, how are you?" Asked the woman serving, she was actually the owner.

"Fine thanks Grace, how are you? Busy as ever I see?!"

"You know it. Can't complain though!" Grace replied. I always quite fancied her. She was very pretty and owned about twenty-five world-wide successful pie shops, what's not to like?! Obviously she was already married. Nice bloke too. She continued "What you having today?"

"Which ever two you recommend please." That was easier than trying to pick.

"Hmm, okay." She turned and asked for a ham hock and cheddar pie and a Cajun pulled chicken and potato pie. "And who is this pretty lady?" She turned back to us and asked.

"Sorry, this is Kelly, she's.. erm.."

"New" Kelly said putting her hand out to Grace. "Nice to meet you"

"Like wise. You're proper punching here Harry" She smiled and gave us our pies. "These are on me."

"Thanks Grace, you're a star! Where's Chad today by the way?"

"I've sent him to the Camden branch; he's in my bad books!"

"Oh no, what did he do?"

She started serving the next customer then carried on talking to us before we left. "Well, I'd noticed we'd started getting lots of birds in our garden and I was happily feeding them. So he came in one evening I asked him to make a bird table."

"Seems reasonable." Kelly responded.

"He's a Aussie and I don't think he knew what I meant, so he made a bird table. It was a list of twenty of his favourite women!"

Kelly and I both laughed and Kelly asked. "That's a joke right?"

"I wasn't laughing," said Grace "especially as I was seventeenth."

"Oh dear! He's lucky he's only been sent to the Camden branch" I said, "when you next get chance try and get him to ask if he's the only *one* you've ever been with, then simply say yes, all the others were nines and tens!" We had a little laugh and we said our goodbyes.

Off we went and enjoyed our gorgeous pies. And for the first time for me, with a gorgeous woman.

I don't suppose it was the plushest food to take somebody for on your second date but she loved it. We sat on a bench in the middle of Covent Garden and shared both pies. Once they were demolished we found a bar. Not long after that, the afternoon became evening and started to become a bit of a blur.

We woke up the next morning in a hotel room. I vaguely remember bargaining our way into this hotel at about 4am. I wasn't paying for a full night considering we'd only be in it for about five hours. Not that this was one of those seedy 'rent by the hour' places like an American motel, it was just off Leicester Square. I think I got the manager down to about £150 so god knows how much it is normally, (probably £99 knowing how drunk we were.)

I do know we passed out after a bit of a fumble, which was a good thing, I'd like to have thought we'd both like to have remembered the first time we actually did the deed. And it was still early into our potential relationship. I'd had enough drunken shags and this was going to be so much more hopefully. What I did realise as my eyes slowly peeled open in the morning was that our room was tiny, and seemed to be in the roof. This would never normally be a problem; in fact, I'd always look for the cheap option on Booking.com. *Do you want to upgrade your room?* Nope. *Extra three-square-feet for £20?* Nope. *Courtyard view only £35?* Nope. Stick me in the fucking basement, that's fine. This appeared to be one of these occasions, a room with a small window and two doors. One door was to get into the room in the corner and the other to the bathroom which was right next to the bed. And I needed a poo.

This was a dilemma; no way was I holding it in after all that booze. I had to go and hoped it wasn't going to be a smelly one. There was no window in the bathroom but I stuck the shower on to cover any unwanted noises to be heard. And I'd jump straight in there after and use as much soap and shower gel as possible to get the nicer smells flowing. It worked thank god. A major embarrassment avoided. I got out the shower and dried myself off, put the towel round my waist and went back into the room. Kelly was awake and sat up in bed. Cover was pulled up and I was trying to remember if she was naked. I should have had a peek when she was still asleep really.

"Wow, that was a long shower." She grinned.

"Trying to wash away my fuzzy head, didn't work though. Shall we go and get breakfast?"

"Yep. But I need a dump first." And up she got, stark naked and bounded into the toilet. I think I was in love.

FOUR

We spent all day Sunday together, breakfast at the nearby café, train back home where she just came back with me. I made us some lunch and we sat about like a couple that had been together years. At about 2pm we decided to go to the pub, she was still in last night's clothes, nothing really dressy as we were out early but certainly too glam for a Sunday afternoon at the local. She lounged about at mine though basically in knickers and one of my shirts, which looked incredibly hot. So we decided we'd walk back to hers whilst she quickly got changed. She lived in a nice flat but said she had to get out of it soon as her landlord wanted to sell it. She told me she might have to move back in with her mum for a while. I didn't know if she was hinting but I decided, sensibly, not to ask her to move in with me. I mean, we hadn't even had sex yet. We left her flat and walked towards the pub, we cut down a street and she pointed out that that's where her mum actually lives, so she wouldn't have to move far.

"Do you want to pop in and say hello?" I asked her.

"No, it's okay. I'll probably go and see her tomorrow; they'd only have a thousand questions to ask you anyway. I can't be bothered, I want wine."

"Okay, if you're sure." I said and she linked her arm through mine and passed we went. *They* I thought? She told me her dad had long gone, who is *they?* She'd only ever mentioned her mum.

I glanced back at the window and saw the curtain twitch and then fall back in place.

―――――――――――

Once we got to the pub, it was my local and, well, I wanted to show her off I suppose. I would normally head down here on a Sunday anyway so it was a bit of a surprise when I walked in with Kelly. I ordered our drinks and after general *how are you* with Kirsty behind the bar, this time involving her smiling and nodding towards Kelly and giving me the good-work-wink, we headed towards the table where my mates were, who had actually just been staring at me, well, I guess more likely, at Kelly, the whole time. I maybe should have texted one of them to say I was bringing someone. But did it matter? Plus I wanted to see this reaction.

We sat down and I introduced them;

"Kelly, this is Ethan and this is Rocket. You two, this is Kelly."

They shook hands and said hello. "Terry actually," Rocket said "my name is Terry, these idiots just call me Rocket but it's Terry, Terry Michaels."

"Nobody cares Rocket." Ethan said and continued after a sip of his pint. "So, Kelly? What's the story here then? We've heard nothing!"

"Nothing much to tell really. I broke down, he punched me in the boob and tried to do me from behind in the first three minutes of us meeting *then* he asked me out."

"It was an elbow. But the rest is probably true." I added with a smile.

"I'm going to have to pop the loo quick, where are they?" Kelly asked standing up.

Rocket, forever the gent, stood up too and pointed her in the right direction. As she was out of earshot, or maybe not quite out of earshot he sat back down and said;

"Fuck me mate. She is *fit!* Where did you find her? I don't recognise her."

"Why would you recognise her?" I asked.

"Yeah right, just because you probably have some sort of database filled with info on every pretty woman you pass in Greater London." Ethan added.

"Well, I would definitely remember her."

"But she is *nothing* like anyone even remotely close to what you could pull I'm afraid pal." I said, rather harshly but he wasn't the biggest catch around. He still lived with his mum, probably a stone or two overweight and would definitely blow a woman off if it clashed with a Chelsea match.

But he knew it. And tended to go for women that would generally get swiped the wrong way on *Tinder*.

"Yeah, but I'm going up in the world. I've got to meet a bird later tonight."

"Bullshit!" Ethan said.

"Seriously, I have. It's that Penny from the chemist."

Ethan almost spat out his drink. "Really? But she's got a head that looks like a slow-cooker. And not the small ones you can get."

"Yeah but I've heard she's a guaranteed bang, so, you know, in for a *penny* and all that."

"Lovely," I added as I saw Kelly heading back over. "It'll be like shagging an empty headlock."

"I mean, a five-litre not three-litre actual slow-cooker." Ethan added before Kelly sat back down.

"You boy's been talking about me?" She asked as she sat back down and put her hand on my thigh.

"Of course." I said putting my hand on hers.

"Why is it," Rocket started "that we can be called boys, and it still seems sort of complimentary but if I say girl to anyone over like, ten, am I a chauvinistic pig?"

"I'm going to the bar. Anyone want one?" Ethan said getting up "I can't listen to these sorts of questions on a Sunday."

"Guinness pleases?" Rocket said handing him his empty glass as we both shook our heads to the drink offer.

"So Kelly, I don't recognise you. You're not from around here are you?" asked Rocket, or kind of told.

"I live here now but grew up in the west."

"What like Richmond or Kensington or something?"

"Like, Bristol."

"Oh." Was all Rocket could muster. He thought London was the world.

"We moved to Oxford after that before moving here about a year ago. Then I got my own place nearly six months after that."

"Who is we?" GOOD question Rocket, I thought.

"Erm, well my dad ran off. He left when I was about two or three so it was just me and my mum," she took a sip of her wine, "and my sister."

"Sister?" Rocket, myself and Ethan as he returned all said at the same time. For different reasons I'd imagine.

"You never mentioned your sister before?"

"Didn't I? Not sure why."

"Older or younger?"

"She's twenty-nine now so, five years older. But she's, I don't know, I little weird I suppose. I mean, I love her and she's great but she's a little bit, a little bit crazy I guess."

"Like clinically crazy?" I enquired.

"No, god no. She's normally normal but she just gets a bit nutty from time to time. For example she split up from her ex a few months ago and moved back in with mum. She just told us calmly it was over and she was back here now. Bearing in mind she was living in Wales with this Dale bloke and had been with him for nearly three years."

"And what happened?" Ethan asked as we all listened intently.

"Well, she'd tied him to their bed, naked. Put that *Veets* removal cream all over him, head to toe, and put makeup on him and plastered photos all over social media."

"That has to be highly illegal, imagine if that was the other way around?" Rocket almost yelled.

"That's not the worst part," continued Kelly. "She had put a chopping board just under his, erm, you know, his bits."

"Oh god." Was pretty much all we could muster.

"Blimey, no, she didn't chop it off but she did staple the bag to the board."

There was a rather quiet minute or two as we mulled it over.

"What had he done?" I finally asked.

"He'd stayed at the pub for an extra pint."

"Jesus, that's a bit extreme!" Ethan said. "I take it that it was about the hundredth time he'd done it?"

Kelly finished her drink and said "Nope, it was the second. But as she said, she'd told him once never to do that again."

More silence as I finished my drink.

"Don't worry though," Kelly said rubbing my leg. "I'm the exact opposite. She got the crazy out of us. I'll get the drinks, same?"

As she got up Rocket asked. "Any chance of setting me up with her?!" and he meant it too.

"I don't think that would be wise do you?" I said. "I'm sure Kelly's sister might want somebody that won't piss her off almost instantly don't you think?"

"Ah bollocks, (wrong choice of word I thought) I'm exactly what she needs, what's her name?"

"My sister?" Kelly asked before starting her walk to the bar. "It's Charley."

FIVE

The next couple of hours were spent chatting away, the lads definitely liked Kelly as I kept getting the nod of approval and I too, liked her more and more. It was approaching 7pm and it was getting to that awkward 'shall *we* go then' moment. I still wasn't 100% sure that if I said 'shall *we* go' she wouldn't just turn around and say that she was staying. It was unlikely but it had happened to me before, and my mates had never let me forget it. This was quite a bit different to that though, we had slept naked together last night, albeit passed out in our own dribble, and this certainly felt like the start of something. I decided to just ask if she fancied getting a Chinese. Good move I was thinking because if she said no I'd just say let's carry on drinking, if it was a yes, we'd definitely be heading back to mine. Turns out she wanted the Chinese and to come back to mine. Phew. The other two said they'd fancy that too but I told them to, well, fuck off.

We finished our drinks, got our coats on and said goodbye.

"Lovely to meet you both." Kelly said and actually seemed to mean it.

"Yes you too," said Ethan, "hopefully first of many get-togethers if he doesn't mess it up!"

"He's doing fine so far." She replied and grabbed my arm before I pulled her in and swamped her from behind in a loving; please don't get a hard-on hug.

"I'm never letting go!" I said in a vomit-in-the-mouth way.

"You had best not!" She replied to make me feel rather good.

"Yeah because if you do, I'm going to catch her!!" Rocket said and laughed. We didn't.

"That's good to know, thanks Terry." Kelly said giving him a wink. "And *remember;* Michael Jackson, if alive and found guilty would have been in trouble for sex with a minor, *not* sex with a miner. Very different issues there."

"Yep, thanks for clearing that up. I did think there wouldn't be a gay miner anywhere."

And with that we got out of there as quickly as possible.

The Chinese was just down the road so we went in and ordered and just sat waiting, watching the girl behind the counter watching T.V despite the rattle of the wok overpowering the sound of the show, (which was, unbelievably called, *Fried Rice Paradise*) every time the kitchen door opened, the girl didn't seem deterred and was gripped by this badly acted show, so much so she sighed every time somebody dared phone to order food.

I was pleased today had gone so well, so many people I know have a girlfriend that doesn't get on with the blokes friends, and vice versa I suppose. It made life difficult. I was pretty sure she'd get on with Claire who had been going out with Ethan for over a year now. We'd suggested meeting up for a meal in the week. Rocket said he'd bring this Penny if things went well, or maybe get Kelly to bring Charley. Both got laughed at.

We got given our food and started our walk back, it would take about fifteen minutes but I didn't want to suggest a cab so we could walk and talk all the way. We did and it was great, but after the initial worry of leaving the pub *with* her, getting food and getting her back to mine I suddenly realised I had the very real possibility of sex. I'd never really got nervous about such a thing but this felt different. Not because she was stunning, even though that didn't help, but I really didn't want to mess this up, and the idea of shooting my load in a matter of seconds after seeing her in the raw was playing on my mind. I was hoping it wasn't going to put me off my chow mien. That was a stupid order though; you can't look cool eating that. Should have got rice or something. Shit, did I order ribs as well?

Turned out none of it mattered. We got in the door and she launched herself at me. I let the Chinese drop to the floor and got involved in the madness of frantic undressing. The sex started on the stairs which is just great for a bit of leverage, before I picked her up and got her onto the bed and it was great, she was great. Fuck it, I was great too! Afterwards she disappeared before coming back with our food and two forks. We lay on the bed and ate all the food, I didn't even care how awkward I looked eating the ribs, after all, my knob was out.

We polished off the food, had more sex, showered (together) then had more sex. We both phoned in sick for the next day and spent all of Monday watching movies, eating and well, having sex. As Monday's go it was probably up there in my top, erm, one. It was around 8pm and we had just finished watching An Officer and a Gentleman when she said she should probably think about going home.

"I haven't got any clothes here."

"You don't need them." My god I was a cheesy bastard.

"I do enjoy wearing your shirts to be fair but I don't think work would like me in one with 2-day worn knickers and not much else do you?"

"Depends, what do you do again?!"

"Not online chat video room things so it's no good!"

"Well why don't we pop back now, grab a few bits and come back here?"

"You not sick of me yet then?!"

"I don't know if that's possible." Mr Cheese was fully here, but I meant it.

"I suppose I could do. But you can't drive because we've had that wine."

"Any chance you could sound a little more excited about the idea?! *Spose' I could do*?!" I mocked.

"I'd absolutely LOVE to I meant to say," a she came in for another kiss. "But how are we going to get my bits and pieces? I don't want to walk, its dark."

"We'll get a taxi; I know a driver or two believe it or not."

"Why don't you get *me* a taxi, ask him to wait whilst I pop in and you stay here and make me some dinner?!"

"You forgot to add *bitch* at the end!"

We both laughed and I got on the phone and sorted a cab. It turned up and off she went whilst I rustled up some food. Just a bit of pasta in a tomato based sauce with mushrooms and onion, some crusty bread and a bottle of red did the job and I sat and waited. I was actually missing having her around, it had only been half an hour but I was actually missing her, and I wasn't just thinking from my pants. In fact, he was knackered and probably deserved a rest.

It got to an hour and she still hadn't returned. I was starting to think I'd been binned and was thinking what an idiot I must be for thinking this was it, she could be the one. What an absolute moron. Surely not, we got along great, didn't we? I'd started to convince myself I'd made a massive prick out of myself before I heard the knock at the door, my stomach did that little excited flip and I think my heart actually high-fived my chest. I went and opened it and she was back! I was so delighted I think I let out a little squeal. I grabbed her and pulled her in for a tight hug. I felt stupid about six seconds into it as I realised she'd only been gone an hour not a year. Am I really so insecure?! I had no reason to be but she already meant a lot to me.

"I had a sudden sick feeling you'd blown me out?!"

"Why would I do that? I've probably had three or four favourite days of my adult life!"

I pulled away from the hug and gave her a proper movie style romantic kiss, where you grab them on both sides of the face and really mean it. And I did. She kissed me back like she meant it before I just returned her back into the hug. My eyes opened and over her shoulder I saw the cases she had with her, no wonder she was an hour.

"Jesus, you got enough bags with you?!"

She pulled out of the hug and looked back and started saying.

"Erm, yeah. About that…"

SIX

We'd sat down to eat, I poured the wine and she started to tell me what had happened. She'd returned home and there was a note from her landlord telling her she had a week to move out. She explained it was a weekly deal they had, which was strange, but it was a favour from a mate of somebody from work and she was just staying there whilst it was being sold. I think she'd told me about this but hadn't realised it would be so soon.

"So," she'd continue, "I thought as I'm packing up a few bits I may as well pack up *all* my clothes and bits. The furniture isn't mine and I'm not fussed about the plates and that, they were just cheapies I bought when I went in. I did bring my kettle though!"

"I guess it makes sense. So what have you got to do with the place now?"

"Well, I'll go back there tomorrow or Wednesday to make sure I haven't missed anything and then give him his keys back."

"Do you want me to come with you? Help you get anything that needs getting."

"You sure? That'd be great. And your boot is bigger than mine."

"Boot?! I thought you'd got most of your stuff?"

"There are just a few more bags of clothes. I am a girl you know."

"You are?! Thank god for that."

We sat and ate the rest of our dinner and drank our wine before I asked the most obvious question that was waiting to be asked;

"So what's the plan now? Have you got a place lined up?"

"I suppose I'll just go to mum's. It'll be fine, Charley is back there now but we could share a room whilst I sorted something out."

"Rubbish," I spurted out, "Just stay here!" Was this romantic or crazy?! Time will tell I thought.

"What? I mean I could do for a couple of days but I'm not sure it's a great idea?"

"Come on, why not? It makes sense. We are going to be spending a lot of time together anyway, hopefully. You'd spend most, if not all nights here rather than top-to-tailing with your big sister." I made a good point.

"I get that. But isn't this quite a big step in a relationship? We're not even officially in a relationship are we?"

"That's easily sorted. Kelly, what's your surname?!" Jesus, how didn't I know this? Especially as I was about to move her in. Again, was this romantic or crazy? Or just fucking barmy!?

"It's Carter."

"Kelly Carter, that's nice and catchy isn't it. You could be an FBI agent with that name. Erm, anyway, where was I? Oh yes. Kelly Carter, will you do me the honour of becoming my sexy, gorgeous and beautiful, loving girlfriend?"

"I'd bloody love to!" She said pulling me in for a big kiss. "But it doesn't count until you change your Facebook status you know that!"

"I'll do it right now," I said as I pulled out my phone.

"You'll have to let me know how much the rent is though on this place, I know this house is big but I'm paying my way."

I put my phone away after rather sadly enjoying changing my status on Facebook. Mind you I couldn't wait to splash photos of us up there. This was how sad I had become.

"What's that sorry?"

20

"Rent?? How much do I need to give you towards it?"

"Rent? I don't pay rent, I own this house."

"Ooh, quite the catch I've reeled in I see. Okay, how much is the mortgage? I'm paying something!"

"Nope, no mortgage either. I own it."

"Seriously? It's a big four bedroom house in London. How?!"

"Long story but I was left it by my Uncle, along with a chunk of money. Hence why I just taxi drive to have a bit of spends. I'm not exactly career driven. I mean, how many 25 year old taxi drivers do you see?"

She moved onto my lap, straddling me so she was facing me with her arms and legs wrapped around me. "None as good-looking as you that's for sure. Such a handsome face."

"Well you know. I grew it myself."

"So, I've bagged myself a bit of a catch haven't I?!"

"I think we both have," I replied and kissed her. She took her top off and asked;

"Hmmm, how should we make this new relationship official?!"

"Well. I've already done Facebook."

"We had best get very naked then."

We did and what strangely went through my mind was *the kettle she brought with had best be a good one.*

The next morning we both woke up early and very smiley. We ate breakfast together and left for work together. I suppose she was my first job of the day as I dropped her at her car. I told her I'd meet her for lunch and give her a key. She was going to take the afternoon off and head 'home' and sort through her stuff. We made room in my wardrobe and draws last night. (I'm pretty sure I'd made some sort of joke about getting in my draws at some point.) I said to her she could do anything she wanted as long as she didn't fill the place with sodding candles.

I spent the whole morning in an exceptional mood. I don't know what some of my regular passengers must have thought. *He's getting some'* was probably the general consensus. I managed to get a key cut and off I went to meet Kelly at a little trendy café in the middle of town. I was there first and ordered a latte and a prawn and avocado sandwich Kelly turned up and ordered the same. Without knowing what I had ordered. It was a small thing but made me smile.

I gave her the key right at the start and we sat enjoying our lunch together. Definitely something I could get used to. We actually agreed we'd meet for lunch every Tuesday from now on. I know we were going to be living together, so therefore, eating dinner together but we decided this would be a nice little tradition to keep. After we'd finished we kissed goodbye after I walked her to her car and she said she'd see me at home! Sounded weird as I hadn't actually lived with a girl before. Obviously there'd been a few girlfriends who stayed a lot but never had I given them a key. Never had I wanted too, until now.

She asked what time I'd be back and told me she'd sort dinner out. I could definitely get used to this. Mind you, she worked until 5:30pm normally where I finished at 5pm, except on Thursday's when I stayed on until 6pm. So dinner would probably fall to me most of the time. I'd perhaps change that depending on how she was at cooking I suppose! I was already looking forward to getting home that afternoon. She'd told me earlier she had less stuff than she thought so I wasn't needed to help move her stuff. Bonus.

It was 5pm and I'd just dropped off my last customer and started to head home. I probably drove a little quicker than I should because I just wanted to get back. I was imagining all sorts of scenarios. I bet she'll be cooking in the buff was my first thought, or hope. Then I thought it's a bit much so pictured her in some nice underwear or maybe just an apron?! Oh yes, that'll do. I pulled up on the drive behind her car and almost sprinted to the door. I opened it up and yelled;

"Honey, I'm home!" Of course I did. Prick.

"I'm back here!" The voice returned.

I walked through ready to grab her into a clench but as I got through towards the kitchen there was a woman sat on my table. And I mean *on* my table, not on a chair. Now don't get me wrong, I don't mind a table sit down, I'm tall and it's easy but would I do it in someone else's house? Probably not. If I did, would I quickly move when I heard the voice of the table owner? Probably. This person instead just looked at me and tilted her head upwards, in a strange L.A gangster sort of way.

"Hello," I said, in a questioning tone.

"Alright?" Was the flippant reply. "He's back Kel. Thought you said he was fit?"

Thanks for that. Luckily Kelly came from out the kitchen wiping her hands on a tea towel and still fully dressed.

"Hiiii," she said and crept, smiling towards me before sticking a big kiss on me. "How did your afternoon go?"

"Yeah good, how was yours? All unpacked and settled in?"

"Most of it. I've left your stuff alone even though I haven't got enough room!"

"There's an empty cupboard in one of the other bedrooms. Use that if you like?"

"*One* of the other bedrooms?" This other person mocked. "Fucking posh twat."

"What was that?" I asked a bit taken aback.

"Turn it into a dressing room and walk-in-wardrobe Kel."

"What was that?" I still wasn't sure what was going on.

"I said she should make it her own room for getting ready in, and keeping her stuff in. Isn't a problem is it? Freddie-four-rooms."

"Who are you?"

"Sorry sweetie," Kelly interjected. "This is my sister, Charley. Charley, this is Harry."

"I gathered." She sort of snarled.

"Be nice!" Kelly said to her pointing her finger. "Be happy for me, please," it wasn't a question.

"Oh yeah sure. I'll just spend the rest of the week farting rainbows hey?" She said getting down and putting her coat on.

"You going?" Kelly asked her.

"Oh no, such a shame. Here let me help with your coat." As I started to lift the coat arm to help.

"I can do it Romeo. And don't get any ideas!" And with that she kissed Kelly on the cheek, gave me a glare and walked out.

"Jesus," I started taking my own jacket off. "Is she for real?"

"Told you." She slapped my bum and told me to sit down, dinner was nearly ready. "And don't go getting any ideas with her!" She said mockingly before heading into the kitchen.

Ideas with her sister? Fucking hell. She was nuttier than squirrel shit. But she was quite hot.

SEVEN

Of course I'm not *that* stupid. I was finally onto a winner and no way was I messing it up. Especially with a psycho family member. But I could certainly see why men would go for her. At least until she looked at them, her stare could kill. But that wasn't my problem and I was getting served a lovely dinner by a lovely lady. Oh Yes, things were looking good.

The next two weeks went perfectly too. So much so we'd arranged to meet up with Ethan and Claire and also Rocket, who was bringing his latest victim, Aimee. We hadn't met her but apparently she looked *'just like Kelly Brook mate.'*

Luckily, Charley hadn't shown up again in this time. She might have been round but not when I was there. It wasn't an issue yet, this potential problem of her not liking me but it would become a big problem in the future you'd imagine. I decided I'd bring it up with Kelly tomorrow. Maybe try and get Charley round for a roast dinner. And their mum, I hadn't met her yet. All hangover depending of course. But for now it was Saturday night, we booked a cab and got dropped at a nice restaurant called Chapter One, just outside Bromley towards Orpington so going further from London, which is probably why I liked it. Ethan, Claire, Rocket and Aimee where going to meet us there as we'd be a bit late.

We saw Ethan as we walked in and headed over. He was sat there next to Claire who stood up and came to greet Kelly. Rocket was sat there, already looking half cut. Next to him was a tall, shaven-headed black woman. Who looked about forty, and pretty pissed off.

"Hello." I said to her but just got a smile. "I'm Harry, this is Kelly."

"Hi," said Kelly giving a little wave across the table.

This Aimee gave a little wave back. "Hiiii" she said in a slightly mocking tone. What was her deal? I'd imagine that Rocket had sold her some fake story or lied about what he looked like. I'm sure we'll find out later.

"Where's the toilet?" Aimee asked.

"Come on, I need to go anyway," said Claire "Kelly, want to come too?"

"Sure."

Don't get me started on that! If blokes go the loo together it's dodgy because it's just weird. Or they're probably off to do drugs, women *can't* go alone. Mind you, after a few beers, you tend to end up on the same piss cycle as another random bloke in the pub, which is fine to start with. *'Alright mate? Oooh breaking the seal? Had a good day? How rubbish are Charlton at the moment? Etc...* But after the fourth or fifth time ending up weeing next to a stranger it just gets weird. You kind of just end up nodding and smiling like a strange relative of Mr Bean.

Anyway they left and we both looked at Rocket.

"What the fuck Rocket?! What's her problem?" I asked.

"I don't know? It was alright at 2 o'clock when we went out but she's just got moodier and moodier all day. Fuck knows what her deal is. I think she was maybe expecting me to just take her to a hotel and give her one? Or it could be that I haven't had any money all day and she's paid for our drinks and is paying for tonight's dinner."

"Erm, the second one I reckon don't you?!" Ethan said. "And she does not look anything like Kelly Brook!"

"Yeah right," I added. "She's actually the *exact* opposite. *You've* even got bigger tits."

"Who said anything about Kelly Brook?"

"Erm, you did earlier when you phoned me to say you were coming tonight with her." Ethan reminded him.

"*Kell* Brook I said. Kell."

"The boxer?"

"Yeah."

Fucking hell, this bloke. Mind you, he was spot on.

The women were returning and at least this Aimee had started smiling.

We ordered our food and plenty of red wine and the conversation flowed well. It was a great evening actually, lots of fun and plenty of little bits of touching between me and Kelly. I decided that she was definitely into me as much as I was her. But that's an easy conclusion after three glasses of wine. But most of the conversation was mainly ripping the shit out of us three men. I got it first;

"What about when you woke up naked in that cornfield in Kent after that outdoor party?" Ethan started.

"Oh god yeah, I'd wiped that from my memory I think!"

"Oooh tell me more, where you alone stud?" Kelly mocked.

"Yes I was alone. But I wasn't completely naked. I had half a bottle of vodka with me and I had one sock on, with a bag of skittles stuck down it. It was tough I was there for about twelve-hours!"

"What did you do for food?!" Asked Claire.

"I had the skittles."

"How did you end up there?" Kelly added.

"The vodka." I said and quickly tried to move onto someone else. "What about you Ethan?! Remember when you put on weight and grew your hair long?!"

"Haha," burst out Rocket, "Yeah you did. You looked like Dawn French!"

"Alright, alright. I was about eighteen and just spent my time getting stoned and eating shit. I soon got myself sorted and now look and feel much better thanks! Also, I wasn't ever into Lenny Henry anyway."

"Neither is she," Kelly pointed out "They split up didn't they?"

"Did they?" Asked Claire. "That's a shame."

"Yeah they did, that's why he is always staying in those hotels and going on about the comfy beds. She kicked him out!" Rocket remarked with a triumphant grin.

The night carried on in this vein most of the time but it was a good laugh. Kelly didn't divulge many embarrassing stories about herself but I'd get them out of her at some point. We were just finishing desert and deciding whether or more likely, where, to go for last orders, when across the table came an almighty slap.

Aimee had slapped Rocket hard across the face; it was quite a whack, very shortly after he'd whispered something in her ear.

"You horrible little man!" And with that she stood up and shaped to go.

"Wow, baby, come on." Rocket went to stand up and we saw how much this woman towered over him.

"Don't fucking call me baby! In fact, don't even call me!" And she picked up his drink and threw it over his trousers, which bizarrely we hadn't noticed were yellow and very tight. And now, very wet.

"Ha well the jokes on you! I taught my dick to drink!"

"What?" I think we all sort of thought and murmured. As he sat back down wiping his crotch with a napkin.

It was silent for a minute. Before Kelly started to say;

"What did you whisp-" I cut her off.

"No Kelly, just no. We do not need to go there. It doesn't bare thinking about."

More silence as Rocket just tried drying his lap with his napkin and finished his drink. He looked up and simply said;

"So, who is going to pay for my dinner?"

"You twat." Ethan said shaking his head.

"Ah you win some, you lose some," as he poured himself the last bit of wine. "So Kelly, tell me more about Charley."

EIGHT

Things carried on really well for the next few of months. I think we had both fallen pretty hard for each other. We spent all our free time together, and even if we met up with others we struggled to keep our eyes or hands off each other. We must have been one of those really fucking annoying couples. But I didn't care. It was approaching four months together by this point and I felt it was time for the next obvious step; Yep, a holiday.

I got home early from work and had sorted a little present for her. It was an old shoe-box and in it I'd put some pictures of a beach, hotel, a pool and all that. Along with a new pair of flip flops, some sun cream and a nice pair of Ray-bans. I bought a matching pair. Told you, we were right wankers.

Kelly came home and I'd wrapped the box and told her I'd got her a little present.

"What's this?" She asked after our welcome home kiss with a big smile on her face.

"Just a little something for you."

"Oh that's so sweet. It's not my birthday til' next week though."

Shit, I didn't think I knew that.

"I know, I know," I bluffed, "but this is just a pre-birthday prezzie to show you how much you mean to me."

She came up close to me and gave me a proper kiss. "I love you, do you know that?"

I grabbed her tightly and said "well, I do now. And I love you too. A lot!"

We had another quick kiss and she took the box over to the sofa and opened it up.

"What is it? I don't get it." As she looked up I was holding the tickets. I say tickets, it was a printed off itinerary which kind of loses its effect. Same with theatre tickets I surprised her with last month. It's never like the movies. *Good news, I've got us tickets to go watch that gig at the O2 you wanted to go to, but I'm out of printer ink so I'm off to Tesco. Oh look at that, the ink is more expensive than the tickets, lovely. You buy the ink and go home and struggle to fit it, don't get me started on that test page, then you finally print them and there's a ten-quid admin charge on the bastard! I'VE DONE ALL THE WORK YOU PRICKS!* See what I mean, kind of loses its magic. But anyway...

"I've booked us a week in Greece. We go next month!"

"Oh my god! Are you serious?!"

"As serious as dodgy mole. I've even spoken to your boss and he's booked you off."

"You sneaky little man you. This is amazing!"

"Well, I thought it'd be nice to get away. Check you out in a bikini."

"You've seen me in a lot less!"

"I know, but I can't show you off naked. In bikinis, I can."

"It's weird but thanks." She picked the sunglasses out and put them on. "Look good?"

"They do! I was actually going to get you a bikini or two to put in the box but bottled it every time I went in the shop. Just felt like a perv."

"I'm quite picky so no worries, I might go shopping Saturday!"

"I'm meeting up with Rocket so I won't be able to come and be dragged around forty-two shops, damn it!"

"Funny! That's okay. I'm overdue a meet up with Charley so I'll see if she fancies it and a bit of lunch."

I still hadn't seen Charley since that first time. I was keeping my distance. I'd even avoided even somehow avoided meeting her mum. Lovely. Until now.

"There is just one problem with this holiday?" Kelly said looking at me.

"What?"

"Well, it's my mum. She won't let me go away with a man she's never met."

"Oh well, Greece is probably over-crowded anyway. We'll go next year." I said heading to the kitchen.

"Oh ha-ha, come on, you have to meet her at some point. Why don't we have her round next week? Oh, I know, maybe for my birthday?"

I'd been ambushed!

"Okay then. I suppose you're right. I do need to meet her. You'd best invite your crazy sister too I guess. At least then if your mum hates me your sister will have stabbed me in the eyeball by dessert anyway."

"You're the best!" and over she came and gave me another kiss before heading out the room saying that she had to go see what holiday clothes she had to take with her. I had a feeling bikinis might not be the only things bought on Saturday.

That didn't bother me. Next week did though. I just had to hope her mum was more like Kelly than she was Charley.

Before I knew it was Kelly's birthday, which meant *the* day of meeting her mum. The day had been great, it was a Friday and we'd both taken the afternoon off so we had a little bit of lunch, in the place we go every Tuesday, even though it was a Friday and that we'd already been on Tuesday this week, we didn't care, it was *our* place and then headed into town. I'd bought her some boots that I knew she wanted for her birthday, she loved them, and I told her I'd got all the hints she'd been leaving. Which was good because I'd probably had bought her like a voucher or something equally as dull.

I'd made dinner and was just waiting for them to arrive. I was pretty nervous. I assumed it was because of meeting Kelly's mum and not because my life could be in danger from her sister. I noticed Kelly was nervous too. Should I be worried about that? Where's that wine?

We heard the taxi pull up and I looked out the window. Charley was helping this woman out of the back seat. It was at the end of my drive but I could see that this lady was quite old. Kelly came and stood next to me and looked out too.

"You ready?" She asked with a deep breath.

"Yeah, you? One question though? Is that your mum, or your Nan?!"

"Stop it! I told you she was old."

"I didn't realise you meant ancient. She looks like the old bird that tells the titanic story. In fact, was she *on* the titanic?"

She gave me a gentle slap.

"Seriously though, how old is she?"

"Seventy." She actually looked more like eighty I thought.

"Seventy?! You must have had dust on you when you were born."

"Don't be gross! And no I wouldn't, she not my real mum."

"What?" I asked as the doorbell went.

Kelly walked off and answered it and in came Charley.

"Heard the good news?" She said before a hello or anything.

"What?"

"I'm house-sitting when you're away."

"What?"

She threw her coat at me and grabbed the wine and drank it from the bottle. I looked at here and again just asked, "what?"

What was happening here?! As the words I were trying to find swirled through my mind I turned around to see this old lady looking at me, from about three-feet away, (and about two-feet upwards.)

"So, you're the prick that's stealing my daughter away?!"

"What?"

"You heard me. What's for dinner?" And off she went and sat down. I turned to Kelly, who was shaking her head, mouthing the word 'sorry' but I just looked at her, then back at this old woman sat at the table tucking a napkin into her top whilst simultaneously picking her nose and the other woman necking a bottle of red wine. All I could muster was;

"What?"

NINE

I didn't say much else at that point, I just walked past them into the kitchen and got ready to start dishing up their dinner, (that I'd spent over three-hours on) I was tempted to bin it all and just do them beans on toast. However, I'm not quite that petty and started to dish up the slow-roasted lamb and Kelly helped me to take the plates out to them. She wouldn't make eye-contact with me throughout the process.

Her mum was called Iris. I'd already decided she was 'Iris the Virus'. I sat down opposite her, which was fine by me but it meant I was next to Charley. Normally at dinner parties, okay, that's a bit posh, normally, when people came around for dinner we'd sit and chat for a while before I served up food but with these two the food was out! Get it ate and get them out.

"This lamb?" Iris asked with a twist of her mouth.

"Mum." Kelly warned "I suggested it because I know it's a favourite of yours, so stop it."

"It is a favourite of mine," she said smiling at Kelly, then looking at me and losing the smile, "when it's done right."

I just smiled and started eating. She was scraping something off hers.

"What are these leafy stick things?"

"It's rosemary, Iris." I told her.

"Well, it looks like they'd get stuck in my pallet." Still snarling a bit. "And its Mrs Carter to men I don't know." Definitely snarling.

But I didn't mind that, I'd quite like to keep it as formal as possible.

"Of course, sorry. Mrs Carter." I said with a smile. I was tempted to add that I'd call her *Your Majesty* if it meant I kept seeing her daughter naked. But I rose above that, for now.

Whilst this was going on Charley was just smirking. She was loving it, seeing me squirm a bit. I really didn't know why or what I'd done to these two fuckwits. Most people liked me!

"The lamb is delicious honey." Kelly said trying to break the awkwardness.

"Honey?" Charley said letting out a little laugh before stuffing a roast potato in her mouth. She spoke through the chew. "Why do you *always* call *all* your boyfriends that?"

I heard Kelly kick her under the table.

"Suppose it's nicer than stapling their balls to something." I added just because I was getting pissed off.

Charley stopped chewing and looked at me then looked at Kelly, before looking at her mum, who had put down her knife and fork and was exhaling whilst rubbing her chin between her forefinger and thumb, and then she was looking back at me.

"What the shitting hell do you think you know?!" Charley sniped.

"I know I wouldn't want my testicles stapled to a chopping board. I think that's pretty obvious."

"Well shut up about it otherwise it might happen!"

"Don't you talk about my boyfriend's balls!" Kelly interjected.

"And don't tell me to shut up in my own house." I was getting braver as I saw Kelly would definitely side with me.

"Don't worry, after what you told me about them I wouldn't go near them!"

"What about them?!" I asked turning to Kelly.

"Nothing, she's winding you up." She said grabbing my hand. "Your balls are lovely."

Charley just started laughing. Then Kelly did. I still wasn't sure if my balls were weird or not.

"Your face!" Charley said pointing at me.

Iris had started eating again. "If I wasn't enjoying this lamb before, I positively hate it now I have the mental image of your scrotal region in my head."

With that, we all started to giggle a bit. I still wasn't happy about it being about my knackers but at least a bit of tension had gone.

We carried on eating in relative order. I'd cleared the plates away and brought out the cheesecake. As I was in the kitchen I was wondering whether to ask about their upbringing. Was I brave enough yet? I doubted it but I wanted to know the set up. How had 'the virus' come about adopting these two, but I didn't know if this was the right time to ask?

"But why give them names?" Charley was saying as I sat down mid conversation. (Hoping they weren't still talking about my balls.)

"Well, I'd imagine it's for meteorological reasons." Kelly responded.

"But it's giving them a face, a name. If they didn't have them, we'd just be like *'oh, another windy day then'* and we'd crack on."

"What are you two talking about?"

"Charley was asking why are storm's given names."

"Oh right. Isn't it so they can be tracked?" I asked after dishing out the pudding and sitting down.

"I get that, but why do *we* need to know the names? Why isn't it just named and kept amongst the MET office or whatever?"

"Because you get storm nerds I guess?" Kelly added.

"Well," Charley took a mouthful of cheesecake. "I wouldn't give it the time of day. I think it gives them unnecessary fame. I mean they never used to do it. Why do it now?"

"But they never used to do the weather?" Kelly said.

"They've *always* done the weather!" Charley replied.

"Well, they haven't *always* done the weather." I said hoping not to rile her and keep it as a friendly discussion.

"I'm nearly thirty and never not known it."

"That's not *always* though is it?"

"Are you saying Michael Fish isn't real?" Iris asked pointing at me.

"Erm.. No, I don't think I am." I didn't even get the remark.

"Okay so maybe cavemen never had a weather channel but it's been going a long time." Charley added.

We sat in a little bit of silence. What could you respond to this with? The silence was about to get awkward before Kelly said;

"Don't even bother talking to her about stuff like this. She doesn't believe that Pandas are real."

"What?" I asked looking at Charley.

"Whatever, when are you going on holiday so I can throw a party and have a threesome on your bed?"

Worst thing was I don't think she was joking. I gulped, smiled and thought I'd best cancel that holiday.

TEN

We didn't cancel our holiday. I'd discussed it with Kelly after they left on Friday. I didn't bother asking how it even came about that Charley was going to housesit but I knew that Charley would have invited herself to do it and bombarded Kelly with abuse if she wasn't allowed. It was an argument not worth pursuing.

The rest of Friday night's dinner went well all things considered. I think Iris started to warm to me and Charley was just Charley. I'd only met her a couple of times but already knew this was a saying. Iris told me to call her Iris from now on. That had to be a good thing. She hadn't said it with a smile on her face or even a squeeze of the arm or anything, she just said it over her shoulder as she left.

I didn't have to see either of them again until it was the day we were leaving for holiday. Charley was due round any minute to grab the keys. One last sweep to hide anything valuable. I'd also decided I was going to dig a bit deeper on this trip to find out more about Kelly's past. She'd never said anything about what had happened to her real parents, she hadn't even told me that she was adopted until Iris knocked on the door. I wanted to know more. I needed to know more. I'd made my mind up already that I was going to ask her to marry me. Not yet, it was too soon, but I wanted to spend the rest of my life with her, I was positive about that, despite her crazy family, but I wanted to know more. There were many questions I needed answering. We hadn't even had the 'exes' chat yet. That was pencilled in for a drunken night though.

Our bags were packed and in the hallway when Charley arrived. I was upstairs hiding my favourite cup. Come on, everyone has a favourite cup; I didn't want mine breaking by this moron. Back of my draws should do. In theory my draws shouldn't even be opened. Fat chance of that though so I buried it deep at the back.

I came downstairs slowly, giving me time to think if I'd forgotten anything. I didn't think I had and said hello to Charley.

"Key?" She said holding her hand out.

"Fine thanks. You?" I said as I handed her the spare key. "No parties!"

"Pah."

"We mean it Charley," Kelly added whilst putting down a bag, "And don't change the locks."

"What?" I asked

"I'm just joking. Right Charley!?"

"Sure." As she kicked off her shoes and took off her jacket. And then her jumper. At least she was making herself right at home.

"What's the pin for Sky box office?" She asked.

"Erm, you won't need that. You've got Netflix and Amazon, so no need to be ordering anything, we'll only be gone a week." I said fluffing the cushions as Charley lay down on the sofa.

"Alright Scrooge."

"Me not letting you order the latest Rock movie does not liken me to a Dickens character does it?"

"Who?"

"Charles Dickens, Charley. I'm sure you've heard of him? Scrooge was a character from a book of hi…. Hang on, you brought him up?!"

"Oh right. Yeah, so he's the bloke that wrote the Muppets Christmas Carol is it?"

"No. Well, I guess in a way, yeah. Fucking hell Charley. Yes, but it was written a long time ago. And not for a muppet movie." This was a crazy conversation and I had a plane to catch.

"Like, as long ago as when this conversation started? Are you going to fuck off or what?"

And on that note we said our goodbyes, maybe for the last time to my house.

The drive to Gatwick wasn't too bad. The taxi dropped us off and we went and checked in. Once we were through the custom checks we found the bar! There's something about having that drink at the airport. Okay, it wasn't quite 10 o'clock in the morning but it didn't ever seem to matter.

We left, surprisingly, bang on time. We landed, got our transfer, again, smooth as you like and we were in the pool at 6pm! And more importantly at the swim-up pool bar by 6.05pm. It was a lovely hotel, nice and clean with gorgeous, blue as you like pools. All Inclusive so we had that magical wristband. We would be friends with every barman by midnight though so it didn't matter about it. Kelly worried about getting a tan line on her back whilst sat up at the pool bar. I told her I was far more interested in other tan lines that should develop.

We spent all week eating, drinking, sunbathing, chatting and well, you know. (Which I'd say with a wink.) My god she looked good with a tan. I was struggling to keep my hands off her and when we had a little frolic and fumble in the pool I'd have to let her get out first as I'd have to stay in the water until something went back down. It was quite scary if a kid swan past, I could have got in a lot of trouble if it brushed someone!

I'd decided well before this holiday I wanted to ask her to marry me. It had been less than six months at this point and I needed to know more about her. Well, not her, I knew most I wanted to know. But I'd like to know more about her childhood and why Charley is so bonkers. I also didn't want to propose on holiday, it was a bit cliché but would try and think of a nice romantic way someplace else, with it still being a surprise and not too cheesy.

It was the fifth night of the holiday and we splashed out and left the complex, don't ever tell me I don't know how to treat my women. We found this lovely little marina-facing taverna which served the freshest seafood. It was perfect. You could imagine us looking like a clip from the Blind Date T.V. show, cheers-ing our drinks and leaning in for kisses and basically praising the absolute shit out of each other but I didn't care.

We'd finished our food and were finishing the wine when I asked her about her mum.

"I was about two, Charley would have been seven-ish and my parents had died in a car crash." She said looking down at her glass. It shocked me as I wasn't expecting it.

"Shit, I'm so sorry to hear that. It's horrible." Wow, that was a bit shit, but what else could I say.

"Thanks. I know it's not an easy thing to respond to, so don't worry about your reaction! And in all honestly I don't remember them or that night at all. Charley obviously does which maybe explains the way she is."

It would explain her being a prick.

"Well it can't have been easy for her." Was my actual reply.

"Pretty dark times." She said and looked close to tears. I couldn't get up and cuddle her because every time I touched her at the moment I'd get a hard-on. I couldn't think of a worse time to get one. I suppose in a playground or something. Anyway, why the hell was I thinking about this?!

"So that's when Iris came in?"

"It was about a year after. We spent that time at my Aunties house, but she couldn't handle the situation so we were put into care. But we were only about a week in limbo before Iris came along. Obviously I don't remember any of this, just what I'm told. But Iris is all I've known really."

Blimey, time to reassess the *Iris the Virus* nickname I thought.

I didn't push for any more details or information as I thought she probably didn't have much else to add. It was quite clearly a tough subject and I didn't need to know anything else. What I had realised is I couldn't possible love this woman any more than I did. The vulnerability she had just shown me made me want to protect her forever. I was definitely ready to pop the question when we were back. It wasn't even six months in this relationship but when you know, you know. This intelligent, funny and exciting woman was hopefully going to become my wife. Even thinking it now sent shivers of excitement coursing through my body. I couldn't wait. And what makes it even better is that she was fit as fuck too!

ELEVEN

Of course, off the back of me delving into her past she had plenty of questions for me too. For example, how was it I was brought up by my uncle? I'd sat and explained about how my mum had died giving birth to me, how my dad couldn't handle that and drank himself to death. I had said to her I think he blamed me for her death, which although pretty ridiculous as I obviously had no control over that, I kind of understood it now I was older. He became an angry man, said things like this shouldn't happen as it's not 1465 and things like that. My uncle was my mum's brother and took me in from the age of three. That could turn out to be an awful turn of events but he was a really good guy, no creepy-uncle scenarios. He had married young. His wife ran off with the bloke that called the bingo numbers at the local hall. From what I remember he was real cheese on a stick. My auntie would have been about forty and this lad was probably just twenty and wore sparkly blazers and bow ties. Not just at work. The best thing was my uncle won the lottery about six-months after the divorce paper ink dried. Not loads of millions but enough. I never knew the exact amount but I know he bought the house I live in and never worked again. His ex-wife tried coming back but he just laughed. That was him though, he wouldn't be a sap. He was devastated when she left, all he'd done was work hard for them, and me, and this was how he was repaid.

He died suddenly four years ago. He was only fifty-two. I missed him a lot.

I told this to Kelly, despite never really talking about any of it with anybody before. She listened and showed such caring eyes; I felt I could tell her anything. It had turned into a pretty morbid evening on holiday but brought us even closer together. That coupled with the fact we got absolutely wrecked on Ouzo, meant we had bonded forever.

The next morning, the day before we were due to fly back, I was up early and headed into town, probably still a bit pissed from the night before, I really needed to jump into that pool and down a gallon of orange juice, which wasn't easy at the hotel, the glasses for the juice were about the size of an egg cup. I'd stand by that jug for about eight minutes in a morning just refilling and downing. What is it about hotels and those glasses?!

Anyway, I'd got into town and found a market stall that sold rings. It would be temporary but it would do the job for now. At least I'd hope so. It was going to be the most romantic part of this proposal. All my plans of flying her out to New York or the Eifel Tower had gone. No, this woman I'd fallen head over heels in love with was getting the real dream. I was proposing tonight; at Stavros's Grill.

The evening had arrived and I was nervous. Luckily, as it was our last night, we both put a bit of effort into our appearance, not that Kelly never did, and she was always looking good. Even in a morning after a night on the booze and she was feeling rough, she had that scruffy but sexy look about her. Tonight especially though she looked amazing. In a tight dress down to just above her knees that hugged all the right areas. I almost wanted to pop the question there and then and rip the dress off her. But I resisted.

We left our apartment and headed past the pool to the restaurant, I let her walk in front of me so I could just to watch her walk. She had the perfect walk, if there is such a thing. And her arse, well. A mate of mine once said that he knew a woman that had an arse like an onion. We were thinking how weird that was until he said *'you know, it makes me wanna cry'*. It always stuck with me but I'd never likened it to the bottom of any girl I'd met. Until now. Her rear was full onion.

We sat down in the restaurant and ordered wine; I didn't order champagne because we had nothing to celebrate, yet. Well that and the fact it's shit. I was sweating but could luckily blame the heat of the country, despite the air con being on full whack in this place.

"Are you sure you're okay? You're looking very fidgety." She said as the waiter brought the wine over.

"Fine. Just hot. Thanks."

The waiter poured the wine and left the bottle in an ice bucket. It was red wine but we liked it chilled.

We cheers'd our drinks and made a toast to our lovely first, hopefully of many, holidays together. As we were looking at our menus I was trying to decide when to ask her. I planned at the end of the meal but I didn't think I could last that long. I certainly didn't think I'd be able to eat. I was looking at this huge menu, all on one big page like these trendy places have now but really wasn't looking at the food on it. I was planning the big question. I'd decided I was going to do it now. Fuck it, let's get it done. If she said no at least I would just sit and eat and drink myself into a coma.

Okay, here it goes. Hang on, I noticed a smell.

I looked up from my menu to see the top of it had been far too close to the candle in the middle of the table and had caught fire.

"Shit!!' I yelled, wondering quite what to do.

I tried wafting it through the air but the flames just got bigger. I was about to jump and throw it to the floor to stamp it out when a huge bucket full of iced water flew at me. I was drenched. Oh, the fire had well and truly been put out but I was an absolute drowned mess. I looked up at the burnt half menu left in my hands, the top half shaped like a mountain range with little orange embers still trying to fight amongst the black singed card and beyond that was Kelly, stood up with a now empty ice bucket. I couldn't find any words. The whole restaurant was looking at us in stunned silence. I just started laughing, Kelly joined in and so did everyone else in the room. Even the waiters, probably thinking, typical British twats. I stood up and went round to Kelly, wiped my soaked face and got down on one knee and asked;

"Kelly Carter. Will you marry me?"

TWELVE

The answer was an instant *screamed* yes and we had an evening to remember. The whole restaurant clapped as I put the ring on her finger and kissed her. Stavros gave us a bottle of champagne, which was vile but we thanked him. We ate our meal without being able to not look each other and smile. I managed to relax after spending the last three hours shaking like a shitting dog and as the night moved on from the fine Stavros eatery we went and had a couple of celebratory cocktails before sealing the engagement with a night of horizontal tango.

The next day we were off back home after a great week, probably my favourite ever I suppose. I couldn't wait to get back and tell people as we agreed not to Facebook anything yet. We were about halfway of our flight back and I caught Kelly just smiling and looking at her hand.

"I will get you a proper one when we back you know?" I said taking out my earphones, pausing the movie. One of the Mission Impossible films, it was quite good.

"You said. But I don't know. I like this one."

"It was like, six-quid or something."

"Yeah but that doesn't matter to me. What matters is that you picked it and I love it."

"Hey, you don't need to convince me. If it saves me about a thousand pound I'm fine with that!"

"A thousand pounds?!" She said looking genuinely shocked, "you'd never have spent that surely?"

"Probably. If they go that high at Argos?"

"Idiot," she said hitting my arm, "I'll just take the cash for clothes."

"Nice try." I said and went to put my earphones back in as she carried on looking at her fingers.

"I think we should have an engagement party, what do you think?"

I thought what I wanted was to get back to Tom Cruise. I dropped my hand and earphones back down and told her it was a great idea.

"I'll get that sorted as soon as we get back then. I'll get Charley to help me."

"What do you reckon your mum and her are going to say?" I was actually bothered by this.

"Hmmm, I don't really know. Imagine my mum will be happy."

"Thank God."

"Not sure about my sister though. She's had a few boyfriends and quite often ends up engaged to them, she was even married once."

"Really?!"

"Yeah it's a long story, I'll tell you about it one day!"

"I'm sure it'll be one to remember, did she end up eating him?"

"Don't be mean. She was young and in love. We can all make mistakes."

"What you going to do if she says she's not happy about this and kicks off, which wouldn't surprise me."

She took my hand and looked at me properly before saying;

"I will tell her that you are my future and I'm extremely happy and she needs to get on board with it or, you know, fuck off!"

"You wouldn't say that to her!?"

"Probably not but I'd make it clear that was the situation."

"That's good. Not the fact you think that but I'd be scared shitless if you told her to fuck off. We'd wake up to dead animals in the bed."

"She's not that bad you know. I reckon one day you'll be close."

"Close to what? Bollock mutilation?"

"Ha-ha, you will be close to that if you mess me about, *I'll* make sure of it, never mind her!"

"As if I would." I leaned over and gave her a kiss. Mainly because I wanted to but I also wanted to finish this conversation about her nutty sister and get back to Tom.

"I know you wouldn't. I love that about you, I trust you."

"Is that it? You love trusting me?!"

"Well, that and everything else! In fact, I don't think I'd change anything about you."

I smiled at that and went to go back to my film.

"Well?"

"Well what?" I asked.

"Would you change anything about me?"

I looked at her and replied, "just one thing."

"What?!"

"Your last name." I gave her another kiss and put my earphones in.

My god I thought, I'm smoother than Ethan Hunt.

Once we landed back at Gatwick we were surprisingly quickly through customs and in our taxi that was waiting. I couldn't wait to get back home; to *our* home now I guess we should call it now, how exciting. I planned to get in, get in the shower and drag Kelly in there with me. Then I remembered; Charley.

Shit, she was going to be there, I'd actually forgotten in all the enjoyment and excitement of the holiday that she was running around at my place doing god knows what. Mind you, I was quite looking forward to seeing her face when we broke the news to her about us getting married. We pulled up outside and I grabbed the cases from the boot and carried, well, wheeled them down the drive to the front door, Kelly was already in there but stood in the hallway looking around. The place was absolutely spotless. I kept a clean house but this looked like it had had forty *actual* super-maids in, not just Supermaids. I was instantly suspicious. What had gone on here for her to need to get professional cleaners in? I was looking for signs when I heard footsteps coming down the stairs.

"Oh. You're back then?"

"Lovely to see you too sis!" Kelly joked.

"This place looks like Kim and Aggie had a three-way with Mr Muscle here, what did you do?" I asked certain of foul play.

"What about it? I'm an extremely clean person thank you very much."

"To be fair honey, she is. Always has been." Kelly obviously felt the need to add. Probably because of cleaning up murder scenes was what I was thinking.

"You need a little more faith in me Harry my boy," as she gave me a little double tap to the cheek before cuddling Kelly. "So, how was it? What a colour you are! Stay golden babe. You though," as she looked at me, "you look a little well done."

"Brilliant." I Said as I walked away.

"You know me Char; I'm all about the good times and tan lines."

"Me too. In fact, I might book a holiday soon. Have a week or maybe two in the sun somewhere."

"I'll pay if you go for a month!" I shouted from the kitchen before walking back out with a bottle of water. "Never know, you might meet your next victim, I mean fella there?"

"Very funny. Anyway, I don't need a man. I need a bikini and a tan."

"Well, get booking." I said before coughing at Kelly to break the news. She looked at me all giddily.

"Anyway, we have some news!" She said as Charley looked at her.

"Oh my god, you're not pregnant?!"

"Pregnant? No."

"Thank god. Mind you his sperm is probably hugely inadequate."

Kelly and I both ignored that. "We are getting married!" Kelly shouted out and hooked her arm around my waist.

"So what do you think about that then, *sis?*" I mocked and gave Kelly a squeeze.

She looked at us. I wasn't sure what she was thinking, her face was stone. It could break into a cry, a laugh or a fury filled scowl. After a couple of seconds she smiled and put her hands to her face and said;

"Oh my god! This is brilliant!! Congratulations guys, as she pulled Kelly in from me for a hug. Then released her and came and hugged me. I was waiting to be bitten on my neck and my jugular spat out in front of me but she simply said well done and continued;

"I know I give you a hard time mate, but it's my little sister, you know."

"I know I get it. Thanks Charley." Maybe I had started to be a little hard on her.

"We should definitely have a party?!"

"We will, as soon as we've told mum, we'll arrange one for somewhere."

"Just have it here?" Charley said, "I can plan it?"

"Erm." Was all I could muster.

"What a great idea." Kelly speaking was quicker than my brain to mouth speed.

"Great. And it'll probably be easier if I just stay in that spare room until then? So I'm on-site for the planning."

"That's a great idea Charley." Kelly added hugging her again. Had I heard that right?

"What?" was all I could muster, again.

THIRTEEN

I felt like that bloke in Jurassic Park, he thinks he has the raptor in his sights only for another raptor to attack from the side. Okay, maybe I didn't want Kelly to be referred to as a dinosaur but I did wonder if this was a hatched plan. Had this been suggested whilst I was on holiday? I didn't think so but wasn't sure. I didn't want to stew on it so I decided to ask her. We were in our bedroom unpacking and sorting washing piles. I hadn't really said much, after hearing that Charley was going to be with us a bit longer, I just walked off and took the cases upstairs. Kelly had followed me upstairs but not brought up what had just been decided. I'd unzipped the first case and started taking the stuff out.

"So...What's this about Charley staying here longer?" I broke the silence.

"What's that honey?"

"Did I hear that right downstairs? She's going to stay here to erm, plan a party? Our party"

"Erh, yes I think it's a great idea."

I carried on putting our dirty clothes into a pile.

"Don't you think it's a bit... a bit sort of unnecessary? Kind of like hiring a live in nanny for your fish."

"What?"

"I don't know. Whatever, look, I don't mind her *helping* to plan our party but does she need to live here to do that?"

"Well, there's no harm in it is there? It'll be handy to sit around over the next couple of nights and chat about it."

"No problem with that. I have no problem at all with chatting about it with her, then, I don't know, her getting a taxi home?"

"Come on, she obviously likes it here, better than having to go back to mums, it won't be for long. It'll give you two the chance to get to know each other better. How much easier will life be if my two favourite people in the world can get along like a house on fire?"

"Interesting choice of words. If I piss her off I'm worried she *will* set my house on fire!"

"Stop being so dramatic. I think it'll be great for us."

It was a pointless battle and not worth rowing over so I conceded. In theory, the idea of us getting to know each other better was a good idea. As long as it goes that way and not the opposite.

"Okay. But just one week maximum. Then I want you all to myself!"

"I'm all yours anyway! This will be fun. And she's pretty well behaved these days," she unzipped the second case, "you know, when sober."

"Wait, what does that mean?!"

"Oh nothing. She's fine, honestly. It's not as if she's a raving alcoholic anyway."

"It's *raging,* but maybe we should make it a booze free week just to be sure?!"

I took my shirt off to stick it on the dirty washing pile. As I did that Kelly came over and hugged me.

"You're so great you know that?"

"Well, you know. I try." I hugged her in closer.

"Wow, you're also like a radiator!" She added.

"You mean because I'm really hot yeah?!"

"And replaceable" came the voice from behind us in the doorway to our bedroom. I turned and saw Charley leaning against the door frame, arms folded. How long she had been there I didn't know.

"Okay, this," I started walking to the door to close it, "is not okay. If you want to stay here you stay out of this room."

"I'm not in the room."

"You know what I mean," as I got to the door I started to close it and she took a step backwards, "and you might want to get some earplugs for night-times!"

I was feeling quite smug with myself for that one. Implying what I was going to be doing with her little sister.

"She still faking it loudly then? She does that with all her boyfriends!" Came the shout through the door.

This was going to be a shit week.

Obviously the night I had planned was no longer happening. Instead of getting Charley to clear off and me cooking our first home-cooked meal as an engaged couple before disappearing off to the bedroom with the chocolate sauce, we instead not only had Charley here but Iris was round. We'd already broken the news to her to which she just nodded with a bit of a *ptthhs* noise before asking what was for dinner.

The food had been demolished and we were sat drinking our wine, or stout, what Iris was drinking. *'Keeps me regular'* was all she'd say when I asked why stout. Lovely.

Of course that wasn't the only time her bowel movements came up through the evening, I learned all about her colonoscopy that she'd had whilst we were away.

"She wanted me to ask for the video afterwards." Charley said.

"We'll it'd be interesting wouldn't it?"

"No mum, it'd be gross." Kelly simply added.

"It's not as if I asked for an external video of them shoving it in love, just what the camera sees of me inside.'

"Drinks anyone?" I stood up to get out of there, "wine? Guinness? Coffee? Food? Sick bag? Ear plugs? Anything at all?"

"You may mock me young man but one day it'll be you and don't come running to me for advice!"

"Erm, okay. You have a deal. Thanks Iris." I disappeared into the kitchen. When I came out a minute or two later luckily the conversation had moved on, a little bit anyway. We'd moved to the front.

"So," Iris was in the middle of saying, "it turned out not to be a UTI but tonsillitis."

I sat down. "Hang on, wait. You thought you had a UTI but it was tonsillitis?" I looked around the table. I don't think the other two were even listening. "Isn't that like, the exact opposite?"

"I don't know love, but I haven't snogged anyone for ages. So I don't know how I caught it. Come to think of it now, I haven't bonked anyone for ages either so that should rule out the UTI as well."

I hid a shudder and decided not to tell her that neither of those things are needed to get them. Nor had anyone said bonked since the war. I decided to change the subject once and for all hopefully.

"Did you tell them what we watched on the plane?" I said it to Kelly to get her talking to these two freaks and to get the subject firmly away from the Iris undercarriage.

"Oh yeah, you two would like it. It was the Lion King but with actual animals, not a cartoon."

"Oh well, I love the cartoon." Charley quickly said. "Does it look like the animals are talking then?"

"Yep, bit like the jungle book they re-did. Really good." Kelly said. They were like a couple of kids again, or at least how I imagined they were like as kids.

"Very clever stuff." Iris added. "The things they do with cameras these days. Amazing."

Apart from sticking them up your arse or fanny you mean Iris. I didn't say it.

"Not only the effects though," Charley began, "but the writers, where do they come up with these ideas?"

"Well, I think the Lion King is loosely based on Hamlet." All three of them looked at me. "Erm, you know, Shakespeare?"

Still nothing.

"What, he wrote a book based on the movie?" Charley asked.

"What?"

"No Charley," Kelly joined in. "He was a writer from a long time ago, this was based on his book, you know, a little."

"Oh right."

"A bit like that, *She's the Man* film, do you remember that film?" I asked.

"Where she pretends to be the boy to play football?"

"That's the one. That's Twelfth Night."

"So Shakespeare liked football did he?"

I was tempted to go back to talking about Iris and her pooper-probe.

"No, look," I started, unable to not exhale loudly, "quite a lot of films that you like probably were a book first. in-particular, Shakespeare. West Side Story etc.."

"Never heard of it."

"Okay, erm. 10 Things I Hate About You?"

"Love it."

"Well that's The Taming of the Shrew."

"Who wrote that?"

"Shakespeare!! Are you taking the piss or what?"

"Sorrrrrry. I just didn't know he'd written more than two books."

"Okay you two," Kelly said and stood up, "to be fair Harry, Charley isn't a big reader."

"You can say that again," Iris added, "she wouldn't even order off a menu if it didn't have pictures on it."

"Let's change the subject," Kelly rightly said, as walking into the kitchen "oh I know, why don't you tell them what you learned was a Welsh word whilst we were by the pool?"

I don't know why I was so wound up because of bloody Shakespeare, I didn't really know anything about him but I knew he'd written more than two books. It didn't matter I told myself, I certainly didn't want to sound like a know-all prick. So I took a big swig of wine.

"Yeah, we met a bloke from Wales and he told us that the word *penguin* is Welsh." I decided I'd enjoy telling people this, I just hoped this Rhys fella wasn't taking the piss.

"But you don't get penguins in Wales." Iris said downing her drink. "Well, except chocolate ones aye!" As she laughed at herself.

"It is a bit odd isn't it?" I said.

"I just realised how it's used in Wales!" Kelly said coming back into the room. "It's in the post office isn't it? You know, when you get to the cashier and you ask; 'have you got a pen Gwynn?'" She said in an attempted Welsh accent. We all laughed. I was so happy to be with this woman. *Despite* the package she came with.

FOURTEEN

The rest of the evening didn't last much longer thank god. Iris left in a cab, on her own. I thought maybe Charley might have had a change of heart about staying here as we obviously were going to spend most of our time banging heads.

She hadn't and disappeared to bed complaining about here back hurting and blaming my dining chairs. I was glad, I was hoping to have a nice quiet evening with Kelly, instead we were only just now getting a bit of time alone, albeit whilst tidying up in the kitchen.

"Blimey," I started with a big sigh, "thank god that's over with."

"Stop it, it wasn't that bad."

"Your mum talked about things going up her arse most of the night. Put me right off my toad in the hole."

Kelly giggled whilst we sorted loading the dishwasher.

"At least you and Charley were bonding."

"Hmm, not quite how I saw it. I think we're destined to row, a lot!"

"I don't think so, we are very similar really, me and her. I don't know, we are like two peas in a bag."

"Pod."

"Pod what?"

"It's two peas in a pod."

"Why is it?"

"Because it is." I don't even know why things like this bothered me. And scoffed playfully as possible and continued, "why would two peas be in a bag?"

"Oh right, I don't know. I always thought it was in a bag, oh well. Every day's a school day hey!"

We finished loading the dishwasher and both had a bit of clean-up of the worktop. How I made so much mess cooking I'll never know. But I did quite like the cleaning up!

"Anyway," she continued, "I think it will be great her being here, you two can really get to know each other, maybe not to start with but believe me, she grows on you."

"Like fungus?"

"Oh ha-ha. Seriously though, I think it will be a blessing in the skies."

"What?"

"What, what?"

I laughed, "do you mean a blessing in disguise?"

She stopped wiping the top and looked at me, "that makes so much more sense!"

"You think?!"

She threw a tea towel at me and said lets go to bed. I certainly wasn't going to argue.

That night though, I was struggling to sleep. It had got to nearly 3am and I hadn't managed to close my eyes and drift off. I'd checked on Kelly and she was absolutely sparko, how she could be this pretty even when sleeping with her mouth wide open I'll never know. I didn't have a clue why I couldn't sleep; my mind wouldn't switch off despite not really thinking about anything. Excitement maybe? I was thinking ahead to our wedding but I couldn't have months of this.

I'd got one of those eye masks that the airline had given us on-board to help me cover my eyes so I had complete darkness, it didn't help. And now I needed a wee.

I got out of bed and headed towards the door, then I suddenly realised it wasn't just me and Kelly in the house anymore, best grab something to quickly put on. I'd slid the eye mask up to my forehead and where my eyes hadn't adjusted to the already dark room I struggled to find anything. I grabbed what I thought were a pair of my boxers off the top of the draws but as I put my leg in them I soon realised it was a pair of Kelly's really tight gym shorts. Oh well I thought, they're stretchy enough and pulled them up. My god they were small. And tight. Anyway, on my way out I grabbed a small towel and threw it around my shoulders.

I dashed to the bathroom, not putting any lights on just in case I woke anyone up, lifted the seat and managed to pull out my mate from these ridiculously tight pants. I was just about finished when I heard the water in bath make that swish sound when someone moves in it. It was still pitch black, I couldn't see anything, I was near a window which wasn't letting in any light but if you were in the bath you would make out the shape of me, and certainly hear me. Why hadn't anything been said, or yelled?!

I moved towards the pull light near the door and pulled down the string. The light came on with clunk and a whirl and battered my eyes.

"Jesus Christ!" I said squeezing my eyes tightly together.

"What the fuck!!" It was Charley's voice.

I managed to regain my sight through a blare and saw Charley propped upright in the bath, Earphones in and thankfully, a lot of bubbles.

"Shit, sorry. I didn't know you were in here!"

"I bet, you fucking perv!" She shouted pulling out her earphones.

"Wait, what? Why didn't you lock the door?!"

"It's 3 in the morning! I didn't think you'd be hanging around waiting to burst in on me!"

"Hardly! I couldn't sleep and came for a piss! Anyway, why are you in the bath at this time in the morning?"

"My back was killing me, a hot bath helps." She then realised how I was sort of dressed. "What the fuck are you dressed as?"

I realised I was stood in front of her in Kelly's really tight lycra shorts, no top on but a towel over my shoulders slipping down my back and a mask on my forehead.

"You look like some pathetic superhero that was kicked out of hero school."

"Goodnight Charley."

"Loser-man!"

"Whatever."

"I can't wait to tell everyone that Perve-man broke into the bathroom to check me out."

"Whatever." I went to leave.

"Yep, really can't wait to tell Kelly her new *fiancé* is only interested in dressing like a washed-out wrestler and checking out her older sister."

I turned back into the bathroom and stood leaning against the door. "Yeah you do that! I was checking you out, and your tits are shit!"

I walked out the door. Straight into Kelly.

FIFTEEN

"Before I ask you about rating her breasts, why don't you tell me why you are trying to spy on my sister in the bath?" She said with her arms folded.

"I know this looks bad but honestly, I didn't know she was in there! The door wasn't locked and the light was off."

"Why didn't you put the light on when you went in?"

"Ok good question. But I never do, I know where everything in my house is and also where everything on my body is."

"And you didn't know she was in the bath?"

"Of course I didn't, made me jump as much as her." At this point Charley came out with a towel wrapped around her but still soaked.

"Honestly Char, I'm only having a laugh. He didn't know." And she winked and nudged me. Not helping.

"Okay I get it. It's just one of those things. We'll say nothing more about it."

I was relieved even though I actually hadn't done anything wrong.

"But why are you dressed like a homeless superhero? Are they my shorts?!"

"Erm, yeah sorry, I grabbed the in the dark. They feel pretty good to be honest!"

"Told you he was a perv!" Charley said returning to the bathroom, closing the door and sliding the lock across, "locking the door!" She felt the need to highlight.

Kelly turned and headed back to the bedroom, I followed.

"Well, that wasn't what I was expecting to wake up to." She said still a bit angry I thought despite what she said.

"I would say it wouldn't have happened if she wasn't here," I said and she went to say something before I cut her off, "but I won't!"

"Good job too."

"Come on, let's get back to bed."

"Good idea. I'm still not fully awake. I need much more sleep."

"I'll get back in with these shorts on if you like?!"

"If you even try that you're dead meat! Get them off!"

"Ohh, you dirty cow, telling me to strip!"

"If you think you're getting any now you've got another thing coming."

I climbed into bed, kissed her on the head and said goodnight. I cuddled in behind her and whispered;

"It's another *think* coming you know?"

"Fuck off."

And we both drifted off to sleep.

The next morning I was in the kitchen with Kelly sorting a bit of breakfast. There were no problems from last night. Kelly said she knew Charley often had late night hot baths with her earphones in and maybe should have warned me. Or maybe just get her to lock the door I was thinking.

Charley came into the kitchen and said good morning to Kelly then slapped my arse and said;

"Morning my midnight superhero stalker perv."

I ignored it.

She carried on. "I was thinking tonight I'd cook us dinner and we'd start planning this party?"

"That's a good idea Char."

"Can't do tonight I'm afraid," they both looked at me. "I'm popping out with Ethan and Rocket don't forget."

"Yeah but you said straight from work, at about five?" Kelly asked in a telling sort of way.

"Well yeah, meet at five at the pub, will be back around ten?"

"So it's like a proper lad's night out then? On a Wednesday?" She let that hang out there.

I looked at both of them back and forth.

"Well?" Charley said.

"What's it got to do with you?! I haven't seen them since I got back. I need to talk to them and tell them my news."

"Aren't we meeting up Friday with them though?" Kelly asked.

"We are, as a couple. I'd quite like to just chat to them as boys?"

"About what?" It was Charley poking her nose in again. I half ignored it.

"Does it matter? I planned it with them before we went away. Rocket will be missing me."

"Just seems strange that you want to go out on a Wednesday with them even though we are seeing them Friday, that's all."

"Not *that* strange, we used to meet up in the week every week. I've cut it back because, you know, I'm with you now."

"Is Ethan the one that goes out with his sister?" We both looked at Charley and asked *what?!* She continued "Doesn't he go out with his sister or something?"

"Erm, no. Where did you get that from?" I asked.

"Kel said, said that Claire was his sister."

I looked at Kelly. "What is going on?"

"I didn't say sister did I? You just weren't listening. I said he goes out with Claire, Claire's brother goes out with Ethan's sister."

I could almost see Charley's brain trying to compute it.

"Still sounds like incest to me!"

"Well it's not, so don't start spreading some weird shit about him please."

"It's far too early in the morning for this," Kelly said, "So you're *definitely* going out tonight then?" She asked looking at me without any chance of a smile.

"Look, I won't normally go out mid-week any more but I want to see them, I haven't seen them for nearly two weeks and I kind of have some big news to tell them don't I. I need to speak to them about being Best Men or ushers or whatever. I won't be late back or even drink that much but I really do want to see them."

Kelly approached me and gave me a quick squeeze.

"You go see your boyfriends then, me and Char will have a girly night and watch a movie."

"Sorted." I gave her a kiss and got ready to go.

"Of course, the longer it takes to plan the party, the longer I'll have to stay." Charley said.

I carried on towards the kitchen doorway, not even looking back. "I'll call them now and cancel. See you at five!" And I left for work.

SIXTEEN

The party planning went well, we picked a date and got things moving. Charley still didn't seem to want to get moving but I thought we'd get the weekend out the way first. Friday was here and we were heading out to meet Ethan, Claire and Rocket. We weren't sure if he was bringing anyone. He thought probably not, but knowing him he would try right up until the last second to find someone.

We were the first at the pub, around about 7pm; we had eaten at home and just coming out for drinks. We found a nice table that would fit all five of us, or six should it be required. Rocket still had about twenty-seven minutes to find a date as we were due to meet at 7:30. Kelly and I decided to get here early to have a little drunk ourselves before the others arrived. It was nice; it felt so good having her next to me. Blokes would always take a second glance at her, it was a weird way to be happy but I liked it. It was normally me doing the double take in pubs, now it was getting done to somebody that shared *my* life and *my* bed. Happy times ahead oh yes. We chatted for the fifteen or twenty minutes before Ethan and Claire arrived. Mainly about our wedding ideas. Although they were mainly her ideas and me nodding.

When Ethan and Claire had sat down with their drinks I slapped Kelly's hand on the table to show her ring. They didn't pay any attention. I coughed and slammed it, gently of course, down again.

"Aherm!" I got louder.

"What is the matter with you?!" Ethan asked.

"Just look at her damn hand."

"I told you!" Claire shouted to Ethan more than anyone else. "Congratulations guys!!" She leaned over and gave Kelly a hug and a kiss then me.

"Yeah congrats man, and you Kelly. You seem to make him very happy!" Ethan said with a big grin.

"What do you mean by *I told you?*" I asked.

"Well, come on," Claire started, "You aren't gonna let this one slip through the net are you. I could see it in your eyes when I first saw you together and I said to him that you'll come back from holiday engaged."

"You said married."

"Well, the next best thing isn't it?"

"I knew she was the one from that first grope under the car bonnet!" I said not sure if Claire knew the story. I guessed not because she frowned.

"Well I think it's lovely, now Kelly, come to the toilet with me so we can pick apart his proposal."

"Yes girls, go and talk about boys with your knickers down. I'll never understand it." It was Rocket; he had just arrived and gave everyone the usual lovely arrival.

"You don't talk to blokes whilst holding your dinky little mate then when you're in the loo then?" Fair point Claire.

"First of all, it's not dinky. It's huge. And second of all, men don't piss next to me because they are intimidated by the size of it."

"Yeah yeah," Claire said whilst walking off with Kelly and wiggling her little finger about. "Not what I hear!"

"Whatever!" And Rocket gave a dismissive wave of the hand.

"Sit down peewee, I've got some news." I said to him, pulling him down on to a stool.

"Hang on; I want to get a drink."

"In a sec, I'll tell you the news and you get us all one. In celebration."

"Engaged or sprogged up? Or both?" He asked matter-of-factly.

"Well thanks for that. Engaged."

"Good. Stag do then. I'll get the drinks."

"He's a miserable sod isn't he?" I said to Ethan as Rocket got up but still in ear shot.

"Because he obviously couldn't find a woman to bring tonight. He's got a point though; we need to talk about a stag do!" Ethan said rubbing his hands together.

"Well, I officially declare you Best Man if you fancy the role?"

"Wow, thanks mate, of course. It'll be an honour." He said and got up a bit to lean over and give me a hug. He sat back down and continued, "where you thinking then?"

"Up to you pal, nothing too extravagant though hey, no Vegas!"

"Vegas?! You paying then?! What about a Magaluf or Napa? Something like that?"

"I think I'm past all that mate. You only go there to pull when you're eighteen. We're not eighteen or need to pull anymore."

"We never pulled when we were eighteen *or* out there!"

"Whatever, anyway I was thinking something a bit more laid back, Italy or somewhere? Or maybe off the scale the other-way and pick somewhere really random like Estonia."

"Okay okay, I hear ya'." Ethan said drinking his drink. "Maybe a quieter European City. I'll have a look and see what I can find." Rocket was back with a tray of drinks.

"We're in luck fellas! Just spoken to my cousin who owns that hotel, he can put up twenty of us if we want for your stag do!"

We both looked at him.

"Where's that then?" I asked.

"Blackpool!"

The rest of the evening was pretty uneventful and well, standard. We talked a lot about engagement party ideas as well as wedding plans. We left at the fairly sensible hour of midnight and we asleep by 1am, not bad for a Friday night I thought. I really was getting old! Especially as I seemed to wake up with a hangover despite not being that pissed.

As we were both feeling a little hazy on Saturday we decided a lazy day was in order? We managed to get Charley to disappear for the day and we vegged out on the sofa watching films all day. It was the evening and we'd ordered a Chinese to be delivered. It arrived in time for Britain's Got Talent, which Kelly loved and I secretly enjoyed.

We were eating our food and watching a dancing dog when Charley came in. Earlier than she promised.

"Don't worry love birds, I'm not staying, just popped back to change into something a little bit slinkier!"

She grabbed a rib off Kelly's plate as she leant over the sofa with her head between mine and Kelly's and ripped apart the rib.

"Umm, these are good."

"Yup." Was all I could be bothered to muster.

"You eaten anything else today?" Kelly asked, "Shall I get you a plate?"

I glanced sideways, probably with a bit of a snarl.

"No it's okay; I'm going to drink my way through dinner thanks."

"Okay then, have fun." I said with a huge hint.

She dumped the bare rib on the edge of Kelly's plate and stood up ready to go upstairs.

"That's such a weird one isn't it?" She said.

"What's that?" Kelly asked. I was trying to ignore her.

"That bird, the judge there,"

"Which one? Alesha Dixon?"

"No the other one. The blonde one, what's her name? Anyway, it's mad to think she'd have had Les Dennis's balls on her chin."

And she went upstairs. To be fair it was a decent point. But it had put me right off my sweet and sour chicken balls.

SEVENTEEN

The next few weeks in the lead up to our engagement party went really quickly. Kelly was being brilliant in just about every way and always happy. Smiling was something that was constantly happening to me too. When I was leaving for work, smiling. Working and coming home, always with a smile. The only thing that slightly dislodged my smile from time to time was the fact Charley hadn't moved out. I realise I'd been played. Played and shafted I suppose. Not by Kelly, I think she was on my side but completely torn, understandably. *I may as well stay until the party might'en I? This w*as the start of the problems. NO! Was my first answer until Kelly worked on me, after Charley had obviously worked on her. Eventually after I realised it was going to be too hard to get her to budge I thought I may as well let her stay until the party was over. *Happy wife happy life* was going to be my motto. And if I'm honest, I didn't really ever notice her there. A meal or two a week and apart from that she either went out or stayed in her room. What she was doing in either instance didn't bother me one bit. Well maybe what she was up to in my spare room worried me a touch, but I'd stick my head in whenever I knew she was out and everything looked fine. And with no more midnight bathing incidents it all went okay.

Everything was lining up. The engagement party was on Saturday (December 14th) at our house, *our* house, still sounded nice, better than *my* house I thought. The wedding was all booked in at our local church for August 8th with the reception at the Bromley Court Hotel, save the date cards would be going out soon after Christmas and New Year. Kelly's hen-do, arranged by Charley was mid-July, Dublin. Mine was at the end of July, where was still to be decided. Gulp. We'd booked our honeymoon though. Two weeks in the Maldives, very expensive but nothing would be too expensive for me to show off my beautiful new wife.

It was Thursday and I was heading out to meet Rocket and Ethan for a curry. Claire was coming around here to have a girly night with Kelly and Charley.

"Got your loose trousers on for all that curry and beer then?" Kelly asked me as I walked downstairs.

"Yup. Got your watermelon and seaweed facial scrub and masks ready?"

"Yup! And cucumbers."

"Oh yeah?" I said like an on-purpose pervert.

"Oh ha-ha." Kelly said giving me a little shove as I got near.

"I'd rather fuck a cucumber than eat one." Charley said from the sofa.

"Why doesn't that surprise me? Anyway, you don't eat the cucumbers; you put them on your eyes." I said getting my jacket.

"You make us sound like *pre-Madonna's!*" Kelly said.

"its *Prima donnas,* it's not something you did before Madonna was on the scene." I unnecessarily said and Kelly gave me playful punch on the arm as I put my jacket on.

"The only time you'd catch me with cucumber on my face is if I've punched a salad. Horrible things." Charley decided to add.

"Okay then, on that note." And I gave Kelly a kiss and said goodbye.

"Them and advocado's, can't stand them either."

"It's avocados." I opened the door and left. Did they do this on purpose?!

I met the other two at our local so we could have a few before heading for a curry. I know it sounds like all I do is eat, drink, go on holiday and meet perfect women. I do work as well though. It's just a bit boring.

Ethan and Rocket, or Terry as Kelly wanted me to actually start calling him; *I'm not putting Rocket on name places and invitations!* She kept saying to me. I didn't really listen though, and I doubted Rocket gave a shit. Anyway they were both already sat down and I made the universal signal across the pub to see if they wanted another drink. They did, I ordered them and mine and carried the three pints of Corrs over to the table.

"Rocket has got some news." Ethan said to me even before I'd even sat down.

"Oh yeah, is that right Rocket? What's that then?"

"Got myself a bird haven't I."

"Another one?!" I replied, "Will this one last longer than a day?"

"Well, smart-arsed, *'I found a girl and getting married within a year'* bell-whiff, for your information we've been seeing each other for nearly a two months now."

"Two months!?" Ethan gasped, "why is this the first we're hearing of her?"

"No reason, just wanted to make sure she was, you know, proper sound n'all."

"And she is then I take it? Do we know her? I asked.

"When do we meet her?" Added Ethan.

"Calm down fellas. No you don't know her, and she will be coming on Saturday with me, To your Party. As my guest. As my girlfriend guest. Yes, as my girlfriend."

"Oooooh, well well, I think someone is in looove!" Ethan teased, "where did you meet her?"

"Erm, you know, around. And I'm not in love, dick. I just like her."

58

"Around where?"

"Around where what?"

"Where did you meet her? Around where? Here?" I enquired.

"Nah, she's not from around here, she's from across the river, Greenwich or something."

"Greenwich isn't across the river."

"Isn't it? Oh, she must have said somewhere else then."

"Well where were you when you met her?"

"Can't remember exactly, no."

"Rocket. What aren't you telling us?"

"Okay," after a bit of silence, "Online okay?!"

"That's perfectly normal these days mate, that's not a biggie." Ethan reassured him.

"Thanks guys. Means a lot to be told that. Told you that I'm not actually that sad and desperate."

"Now now, we didn't say that did we?!"

We sat and chuckled whilst having a sip of our drinks.

"It's just," Rocket started, "ah nothing."

"No go on mate, what is it?"

He took another sip, like he was bottling up the courage to tell us he loved this woman or something.

"It's just that it wasn't a *normal* website if you know what I mean?"

Ethan looked at me before saying, "no Rocket, we don't know what you mean. In what way wasn't it normal?"

"Well I got told about it from a bloke I speak to on the train most days."

"Not fucked up Phil?"

"Yeah, fucked up Phil."

"Oh god, what's the website Rocket?"

He took a big sip of his drink as we waited to see what gem was due to come out of his mouth. We weren't disappointed;

"It's for amputees."

Ethan spat out his drink as I put my hand to my head.

"It's not like it sounds," he continued, "honestly. I've not done anything wrong."

"In what way is it not like it sounds?" I asked.

"Do you have to be an amputee to be on this website"? Ethan followed up.

"Erm, yeah."

"So it's exactly how it sounds." Ethan added.

"Rocket?" I started, "you're not an amputee."

"I know."

"So how are you on it?"

He drank another big gulp of his beer. "I've said I've got a foot missing."

"Jesus Christ. This is a new low Rocket, even for you!" Ethan said.

"It's okay though, fucked up Phil gave me a picture of his leg with his foot missing. You had to send proof you see."

"How do, erm... what does.. why do... erm. What?" Was all I could muster.

"What's the big deal?" He asked unmoved.

"Did you know fucked up Phil had a missing foot?"

"No you see that's the beauty of it. You wouldn't know by just looking at him, that's what gave me this idea. Genius I reckon."

"Give me strength." Ethan said and got up to get more drinks.

"It's not *that* clever though is it mate? Have you had sex with her yet?"

"Yeah, sorted that straight away like. Even though she's quite religious. Still got through."

"Yep so anyway, *how* has she not seen that you don't have a foot missing?"

"What do you mean?"

"How the fuck are you going to get away with having two-feet? Tell her one grew fucking back?!"

"Oh I see what you mean? Hadn't really thought about that. I'll just keep leaving my trainer on? Told her I'm embarrassed by it."

"That'll be good if you are with her for a few years wont it?!"

"Ah we'll cross that bridge when it comes to it." He said as Ethan returned and sat down.

"Soul destroying you are, in this instance *actually* soul-destroying. Hang on; this is an amputee dating site yeah?"

"That's right," as he drained his pint, "why?"

"Why? Well what the hell has she got missing from her?"

"Oh yeah. Erm, her arm."

"Her arm? Jesus. What happened?" Ethan was getting up to speed.

"Not really sure, she said she lost it in Na'am."

"NA'AM?!" Ethan and I said loudly together.

"Fuck me, how old is she?"

"I don't know, why, when was Na'am then?"

"Like, throughout the whole of the 60's!" I struggled to keep my voice low.

"So she's what? Sixty-odd?!" Ethan asked.

"No! I'm not a weirdo you know!" We weren't sure, "she's only twenty-four. Is she winding me up then?"

"Fuck me Rocket, yes she's winding you up."

"Ah right. She has got a good sense of humour. When she said to me about Na'am I just asked if she meant Na'am as in, *haven't got*"

"What?"

"You know, haven't got... N'arm. That's how she is."

This conversation was getting weirder by the second...

"Well I can't wait to meet her. Good god, we'll have to remember that you only have one foot won't we. Which foot is it?"

"Which foot what?"

"Fuck me Rocket, which foot is supposed to be missing?!"

"Oh right, yeah, erm not sure, think it might have changed a few times, it's hard to remember when you're getting down to it. Anyway, which curry house we going to?"

"You're a terrible human being Terry, you know that? Usual one?"

"Yep, good with me. By the way Rocket, what's she called?"

"Oh right yeah, Mandy. Mandy Tapp."

Definitely didn't ring any bells with me or Ethan.

"Nice name," I said. "Bet she's easy to turn on?"

"Or off?" Ethan added, "is she a hot one? Or cold?"

"Yeah she is, hot, I mean. Why?" Rocket didn't get the joke, as usual.

I decided against a tapping-that-ass joke and we finished off our drinks and headed for the curry house. I'd had enough weird conversation for one night. Bring on Saturday; if nothing else, I was intrigued to meet Ms Tapp.

EIGHTEEN

The party was here and we were excited about it, me especially as I was getting to show off Kelly to everybody that didn't know her yet, and rub her in the noses of my mates that did. I wouldn't call it petty, well, maybe I would but I didn't care, I was just mad about this woman and it just so happened she looked like the younger sister of Gal Gadot. Yes, she was my very own wonder woman.

It was about 7pm when the guests were due to start arriving. Charley, to be fair, had done a good job. I was looking forward to kicking her out but I couldn't fault her on sorting this. The place was decorated perfectly; she'd told me the people she'd invited to get my approval and even used a catering firm to do the food. It cost me enough but I wanted it to be perfect.

It was just gone 6.30pm and I had to pop from the bathroom to the bedroom for something and I saw Kelly just finishing off getting ready in our room. I was about to walk in and just pick her up in a big hug, slap a big kiss on her and tell her how happy I was, but instead I stayed just outside the doorway and watched her. Magnificent I thought was the only word I could find to describe her. Not just because of how she looked but the way she was, she was smiling and singing along to whatever was on Alexa and looked lost in her own little world, she glided. I hoped the smile was because of me and our future life. My Uncle would have told me she is just a lucky as me. I wouldn't see it that way. I'd always found myself with a more Marilyn Manson type than Marilyn Monroe type women but I'd finally realised why. I was getting saved for this woman.

I was just stood watching and thinking how the other three men, she told me that's honestly all there'd ever been, but I was wondering how any of them could let her slip through their fingers. Who knows? Who cares? Their loss was definitely my gain. I was about to walk in and tell her how lovely she looked when Charley popped up behind me. Not saying anything at first. Before making me jump with words;

"Pretty darn hot isn't she."

"Jesus, how long you been stood there for?"

"Long enough to watch you watch her. Don't worry, not in a seedy way, I can see how much you love her."

"That's good to know, and you won't get an argument from me!"

"You do know if you hurt her, I *will* kill you?" There was no jest in her voice.

"I know," and I did, "but you know there is absolutely zero chance of that?"

"I thought so, just checking. And don't worry, I don't want you to be on tenderhooks around me all the time, you're not all that bad. Letting me stay here for free is good of you. I'll hopefully get a place sorted early next year. Definitely by the wedding."

"Thanks Charley, I just want you to know how great of a job you've done getting this party…" It hit me what she said, "what did you say?"

"I need to stay a bit longer, did Kelly not tell you?"

"Hasn't come up…"

"Well, don't shoot the messenger!"

"Messenger?! Charley, you're the package!"

"Why thank you very much."

It was getting nearer 7pm and I didn't want to get involved in a row, she would definitely kick off and ruin the party, no way was this squatting happening but it could be sorted easily tomorrow, I went for the diplomatic approach for now.

"Well we'll have a chat tomorrow hey? Oh and thanks for sorting the party, everything looks great." I said with actually sincerity but also in a smoothing over sort of way.

"No probs," she punched my arm, "bro!"

Jesus. "Oh and thanks for your kind words about me admiring your sister, I do really love her, I didn't realise it showed all the time though for others to see. How could you tell?"

"I can just see it in your eyes. I think everyone can." With this she turned and walked off.

"Oh right, thanks Charley."

She spoke as she walked away towards the stairs, she didn't look back and said "Well, the eyes. And the fact you haven't got any trousers on and your erection was blatantly obvious."

I looked down and saw I was missing trousers. But least my hard-on had gone.

Shit. That's what I was going to the bedroom for. Now I remember.

"It's *tenterhooks* by the way!" I shouted over the bannister trying and failing to claw back some dignity, but she just ignored me. As I would have done too. I needed to stop doing that!

The party was going really well, everyone we expected to come had, as well as a few that we hadn't expected to come, but it wasn't too bad. It's not as if Charley had put it on Facebook. Yet.

Kelly and I were working the room I guess you'd say. We had a big marque out in the garden with heaters, seating and a bar. Oh and a band, just a local quartet but they were very good. They were called the MCB. I didn't know what it stood for but they played good stuff, even if the lead singer was a bit of a twat.

I was just heading to the bar to get a drink and the fact I saw Ethan there talking to another mate of ours called Dean. There was still no Rocket yet, it was getting towards 9pm.

"No Rocket yet then?" I asked the other two and then asked the hired, rather good-looking barman for beer. I don't know why I picked up on that. I'd just make sure I'd get Kelly's drinks from now on. I wasn't insecure but this bloke and Kelly would have ridiculous children.

"Not yet," Ethan started, "but he's text a while back to say to say he's left."

"With Mandy Tapp do we know?"

"Alone. Apparently they had a row last night, he called her Mandy-capped and that was that."

"My god that bloke. What is he like?!" I was finding myself saying yet again.

"Anyway, we can rib him when he's here, Dean, tell Harry about your gym boyfriend, this will make you laugh." Ethan said smiling.

"Do I have to?" Dean asked.

"You may as well otherwise I'll tell it and exaggerate it to a bumming."

"Okay, alright. Well, I have this personal fitness guy at the gym, Frank." Dean started. He was only about five-foot-five Dean and fought constantly to build up his stocky frame with Dolph Lundgren style muscles. And was failing.

"Frank?" I asked. I didn't know him.

"Yeah, Frank. Now Frank is about six-foot-seven, black, solid as a rock and extremely gay."

"Okay."

"He's very good though, really gets you going through your paces, but he does this thing, when you are finished on one machine, he grabs you by the hand and sort of walk-runs you over to the next machine. You know, a bit like that bald bloke from the Crystal Maze used to do. I don't know why, it's just what he does and it's never a problem."

"Right," I didn't respond much as I didn't know where this was going.

"Well," Dean continued with an exhale, "today I was on the treadmill and from there he usually takes me over to the chest press, which is nearby, but today he wanted me to go to the rowing machine which is right over the other side of the gym, and you know how big the gym is. So he grabs my hand like normal, and I mean grabs it, interlocked fingers and everything, anyway we start walking, not running, across to the rowing machine when he stops to speak to a woman halfway across who has just walked in, and she's fit."

"So?"

"So, I'm stood there holding hands with this huge, gay bloke whilst he's talking to this woman. I'm just there holding his hand, looking around, not knowing what to do! He spoke to her for nearly fifteen minutes! Honestly, it must have looked like something from the Blue Oyster bar."

"Why? What were you wearing?!" Ethan asked.

"Well, not leather but you get what I mean."

"You'll have to take him some flowers when you next go, holding hands, making plans."

"If you think I'm going back there you've got another thing coming."

"Think coming." I was doing it again.

"What?" Dean asked as we saw Rocket making his way through towards us.

"I've already had this conversation with you and several others. It's, *you've got another think coming*, not thing."

"No it's not, who says that?!" Dean said and meant it.

"We'll obviously not you, Bromeo."

"It doesn't make sense though; you've got another think comi... Oh, hang on... I think you might be right actually. I've always said thing. How bizarre."

"I think most people do pal."

"Or you thing most people do?!" Dean said and laughed just as Rocket joined us with a drink handed to him by Chris Hemsworth behind the bar.

"Jesus, where did you find him?" Was the first thing Rocket asked. "Marvel-lous men hire or something?"

"I didn't hire him did I numb-nuts, as if I would, mind you, maybe I hired him for Dean here, you know; now he's gay."

"Fuck off, bunch of pricks." Dean said laughing and walking off.

"Say hi to Frank for us!" I shouted after him.

"Yeah, in the morning when you wake up together!" Followed Ethan.

"What's that about?" Asked Rocket.

"Oh nothing really," I told him, "so, what happened to Mandy then?"

"Huh? Oh right, yeah I binned her."

"Oh right."

"Yeah, not that fussed anyway," but he was definitely bothered by it. "She looked like a packet of ham."

We didn't even have the slightest idea what that meant but we saw that Charley was heading over our way so we didn't push it any further.

"Look out, it's the Artful Lodger." Quipped Ethan as we noticed Rocket flattening down his shirt and breathing in.

"Hello boys." She said in playful way which instantly put us on edge. "Rocket, where's, erm, *Mandy can't Clapp* or whatever her name is? Can't wait to meet her."

Maybe Charley and Rocket did actually suit each other, both about as shallow as a bird bath.

"We broke up, so I'm yet again, young, single and free to mingle." But it wasn't said with the usual way that he would say it. The 'umph' wasn't there, or even the edge of desperation.

"I bet you are, and there will be a really lucky lady out there for you somewhere, I have no doubt whatsoever," Charley replied slapping him playfully a few times on the cheek, before clocking the bartender's eye and getting ready to head over. "I mean, how old will those women from Chernobyl be now? Possibilitieeeees!!" And with that she was off, before stopping and turning back, "Now there's an idea, possibilities for disabilities, I'm setting that up." And she headed back towards the bar, or should I say, *barman*, screaming at him to pull her a drink and then pull her.

"She's an absolute diamond that one." I said with severe mockery.

"You can't believe her and Kelly came from the same set of balls can you?" Ethan added.

"I like her!" Rocket said. "I'm going to be in there by the wedding I bet you."

Ethan and I just laughed, we weren't sure if he actually thought he would be. He seemed a little cut up about this Mandy girl, by his record they had been together on a while. As for going after Kelly's sister, it just made me laugh. I mean Charley is a pretty vicious woman, well, from the little I knew about her and my actual experiences of her but she was still a very good looking woman, and therefore, way out of his league.

Anyway, I explained to them that the balls in question, that these two were started from probably weren't the main issue, and they'll soon have the pleasure of Iris the Virus. '*Is she fit?*' Rocket asked. I told him she was seventy and he just asked the question again. I think his reasoning was that she had two extremely attractive daughters so she must be hot herself, Helen Mirren hot he called it, or as he pressed the issue, he said Sophia Loren is hot and she's over eighty! I explained that Iris looked more like Ralph Lauren but stopped short of telling them that she wasn't their real mother, that wasn't my story to tell. Maybe their real mother *did* look like Sophia Loren!?

"Anyway fellas, I need to have a chat with you." Rocket said, "important like."

I highly doubted this. Rocket's idea of important was if he should subscribe to *Pornhub* or *RudeTube*. (He subscribed to both.)

"Sure mate, what's up?" Ethan asked.

"Well, this Mandy I've been seeing…"

"Yeah?" We responded together as we listened.

"You know the one with one arm?"

"YES Rocket, we know the one."

"Well, we had a row." My god, this was going to take a long time.

"Yep, what about?"

"She told me that she's, erm, sort of pregnant."

We were a little lost for words. I stumbled to a question; "Erm, mate, I don't really know what to say. Have you spoken to anybody else about it? What to do?"

"Of course I did. First person I asked what to do was Siri. She was shit."

I was about to say something else when Rocket spotted Kelly heading over.

"Shh, Kelly's coming, we'll talk later," he said.

"Shit mate, what the fuck? This is crazy!" I quickly added.

"Shut up, we'll talk about it in a bit!"

"We should ask Kelly about it." I added.

"No way!" Rocket spouted back.

"No, he is right mate, honestly, ask her about it, woman's view will definitely help here, I mean what do me and Harry know about it?" Ethan added.

"He's got a point. Plus I will probably just tell her later anyway." It was a fact, pointless pretending otherwise.

He thought about it for a few seconds, but shook his head as she came up and stuck her arm around my waist.

"Hey boys? How are we doing?" As I bent down to give her a kiss.

"I got a one-armed girl pregnant!" He blurted it out.

It was quiet for a few seconds. Ethan was looking down into his drink and I was looking everywhere around the room trying not to make eye-contact with anybody, whilst Kelly just looked at him. Rocket was biting his thumb nail; either that or he was sucking his thumb. He honestly looked about ten years-old, I'd never felt more sorry for him.

"Okay," Kelly started and paused, "how, I mean, what happened then?"

"We had loads of sex and now she's pregnant."

"OOOH, who is?!" Oh no, Charley was back in ear-shot and overheard.

"Nobody Charley, go away." Kelly said.

"No way, I want to know!" I wasn't sure where she got this, *I know you all well enough to act like this* with us from, I suppose it was just who she was.

"I did." Rocket said.

"Congratulations stud. A little Rocket, or should I say, a littler Rocket running around hey? Good god. You see, if you had a girlfriend with two arms you wouldn't be in this mess, she would probably have just wanked you off."

"CHARLEY!" Kelly shouted at her, "Leave... NOW!" I'd never heard her raise her voice, I quite liked it. Especially as it was aimed at Charley.

"Alright, alright. Whatever. Who cares anyway? Just let me know if you want me to push her down the stairs or anything."

She headed back to the barman, thankfully.

"Right Terry, let's sit down," Kelly led him over to the table and we all sat down, she sat next to him and took his hands, "sorry about her, she's all about effect, she won't mean any of that." We weren't convinced by that though. Kelly continued. "So, she is definitely, you know, with child?"

"It's not Downton Abbey Kelly. Yes, she is definitely, definitely up the duff. We did two tests and she has been to the doctors, she's seven-weeks."

"And when was this?"

"Yesterday she told me and I made her do more tests."

"Okay, okay. That's okay. Erm, now then. How was it left?"

"I freaked out and told her to get rid of *it*! I didn't know what else to say, I don't want a baby, no way am I ready. Neither is she, I told her *it* needs to go"

"And how did she react?"

"She screamed at me and told me she didn't want to, never ever would she and couldn't anyway."

"Why not?" Ethan asked, out of curiosity nothing more.

"She's really religious. Said it's against her beliefs and the beliefs of her family, Jesus wouldn't approve and all that sort of rubbish."

"That's mental isn't it?" I butted in.

"What is? Religion?" Kelly asked.

"Well, I mean, come on, people passing judgement, spouting off about surprise babies because of Jesus, a bloke that came from *the most* famously unplanned pregnancy ever?! Give me a break." Valid point I thought I was making.

"I think we'll save this discussion for another day maybe huh?" Kelly suggested shutting me down, before talking to Rocket again, "so how was it all left?"

"I tried getting her to leave but she wouldn't go."

"Why not?"

"It was her house."

"Rocket! You're such a knob. So did you leave?" Ethan asked.

"Yeah, I didn't know what else to do, so I called her a name and I just left. I've got loads of missed calls from her and her mum."

"Do I want to know what name you called her?" Asked Kelly.

"No." Ethan, Rocket and I all said at the same time.

"Okay then," Kelly started,"erm, well you're going to have to speak to her Terry, a very serious discussion is needed with her. If she is keeping the baby, which seems almost certain, you'll need to figure out what role you are going to take..."

"But I don....." Rocket tried to say something but Kelly didn't let him finish.

"Figure out what role, if any, you want to take in bringing up this child. You need to think long and hard. It's hard enough being a single mum, but a single mum with one arm? We'll I don't even know where to put that in the line of toughness. Very near the top."

"So you're saying I need to man up and do my bit?"

"Well, I'm not telling you what to do at all, it's your decision obviously, and I'm just *advising* you to not make any rash decisions now. You only found out yesterday, of course it's a shock, but it's not like you're trying to decide whether to buy the Chelsea home kit or away kit this season, it's a big, big, huge decision. If, of course she wants you to be part of it, which by the looks of it, she does. Try putting yourself in her shoes. How scared you are? Times that by ten."

"Speaking of shoes though," Ethan interrupted, "how are you going to explain that you actually need two?"

"What's that mean?" Kelly asked.

"Nothing!" Rocket blasted, I think he had enough to deal with without getting shit for this, for now. "Thanks Kelly," he kissed her gratefully on the hand, a bit like she was the Pope for some reason, "and by the way, I get both Chelsea shirts."

"That's great Terry. Great focus there."

"Hey Rocket, maybe she will have a boy!" It was Charley heading back over; couldn't this barman string a sentence together or something? Not that I think Charley was into him for his conversational skills.

"Oh Jesus, I'm not ready to think about it yet, I need to get pissed."

"That'll help!" Charley said as she stood next to us.

"Haven't you got a barman to swoon over?" I asked her.

"Swoon? Alright Grandad, I was just going to say that Rocket needs to be quick if he wants to get pissed before talking the one-armed girl again, okay?"

"And why's that?"

"Well, she's just walked in."

NINETEEN

The evening had obviously taken a turn. I felt sorry for Rocket, I think. I did because he was a mate but this whole relationship was surely just wrong from the beginning. He lied about having a missing foot so god knows what else he lied about to get this apparently devout Catholic into bed. I made a mental note to check this out with him. Kelly was great in her advice for him but if all he's done is lie surely this poor girl will run to the hills. He's a really nice bloke but he would do anything to try and get his end away, mind you, this was probably the worst I'd known. He'd gone off with Mandy to talk things through. He'd gone upstairs for a bit of privacy. God knows what the outcome will be? I just hope they sort something out. I'd find out later no doubt. But my evening was about to take a personal nose-dive. Iris was heading my way. I'd done well to keep it to a brief hello and taking her the odd drink, but now she was heading over with Charley on her arm, both scouring at me for some unknown reason. What was their problem?

She said as she sat down opposite me across the table. I was alone, where the hell was Kelly?!

"It's like the bloody *artic* out here." Start with a moan I see.

"What? In this lorry?"

"What?"

"Nothing, how are you enjoying the evening Iris?"

"I'm not."

"Oh dear, why is that then? The band not playing your jam?"

"What did he say?" She asked Charley who had sat on the seat between us.

"Nothing mum, I *think* he's trying to be funny."

"I'll find my sense of humour once you move out, *sis*." I lingered on both the ess's of that word.

"Funnily enough, that's what we came over to tell you, I'm moving out, tomorrow probably."

"What?!" I sprung forward in my seat, "seriously?!"

"Yep." I was lost for words, if it hadn't been a free bar I'd have bought everyone a drink, which I suppose I was already doing, anyway, my excitement didn't last long. "Mum is going to move in, in my place whilst I go back and sort out her house."

I basically burst out laughing. "Good one, seriously though, you are going yes?"

"Yes, seriously, and I'm serious about mum. She can't be in the house with all those paint fumes."

"What paint fumes? What are you talking about?"

"Didn't Kelly tell you?"

"Tell me what?"

"Oh you'll have to ask her then."

"Charley. Just tell me!" I was shouting but I was definitely agitated.

"No way, but I'll go get Kelly so I can watch whilst she tells you."

"Don't bother, I'll go and find her." I stood up as quickly as I could, looking at these two morons, Charley was just drinking her drink through a smirk and winked at me and when I looked at Iris she was just chewing on a whole cucumber, I don't even know where she got it from but she was eating it side on like a corn on the cob.

I left the marquee, (which was actually quite warm I thought) and headed into the house, Kelly wasn't in the kitchen or around the dining table, or in the front room. I headed upstairs and checked our room, still not there. I went into a spare bedroom and saw Rocket and Mandy lying on the bed snogging the faces off each other, at least that looked like a decision had been made; it was now me that looked like decisions were on the agenda, hopefully ones including me! I didn't check Charley's room, Charley's room?! Fucking hell, MY spare room I meant to say, and headed to the fourth, smallest room which I kept as a study, I say study, it had a few books in and a PC so I could play football manager, which I'd actually been forbidden to play by Kelly. It was a harder sacrifice than you may think. Anyway, the door was ajar and the light was on. I went in and saw Kelly in there;

"Alright?"

"Jesus! You scared the life out of me!" Kelly replied putting her hand to her chest.

"Sorry, what you doing in here? You're not a secret football manager fan are you and you're getting your secret fix?"

"Good god no, I'd rather shit in my hands and clap than play that. No, I just popped in here to get the spare phone charger but I can't find it."

"You lost yours then? At a party?"

"No, mine is by the bed but I don't want to give that one to Mandy in case I don't get it back."

"I think something else is plugged into Mandy now so I wouldn't worry. I assume you're the reason they are *all friends* again in there?"

"I made them see the positives yes but left them to talk whilst I got her a charger."

"Well they're done with the talking. But I don't think we are?"

"Ooh really? *Mr something on my mind*, pre-tell."

Now, this was a delicate situation, I mean, it shouldn't be. If Kelly wanted to move her mum in, however temporary, surely it's a discussion that we'd have together first. But I knew how much Kelly loved her mum and sister and would probably just see it as helping them out and I really did want her thinking this was her home, so to make decisions without involving me. Obviously, I had this in mind if she, I don't know, wanted to change the curtains, fine. Maybe get a new kettle, yep. But things like, get a dog, that's a joint decision. Buy a new television? I'd like a say. Move a dusty old crow in? TALK TO ME FIRST!

"Charley just mentioned that she's moving out?"

Kelly looked busy looking through stuff so she didn't have to make eye contact.

"O-herm, yep." Still not looking at me.

"That's good isn't it? Get the house back to ourselves."

"Yep, lovely."

"Be nice and quiet again, just me and you."

"Can't wait, yep."

"What shall we do tomorrow to celebrate, naked scrabble?"

"Sure, good idea."

"Why the fuck is your mum moving in Kelly?!"

She stood up and threw her arms around me, "I'm soooo sorry! They ganged up on me and backed me into a corner!"

"Well I'm going to un-back us out of said corner!"

"Un-back, is that a word? Did Hanson sing it?"

"Kelly, don't try and make me laugh, this isn't happening!"

I went to leave but she wouldn't let go. "Please Harry, I'm really sorry but it's just for a week whilst Charley decorates the house, we won't even know she's here, I promise."

"I find that hard to believe! She going to cook for herself? Jesus, does she even still piss for herself?!"

"Yes Harry, she's got all her functioning organs still! And dinners? I'll do all week."

"Bloody hell." It's all I could muster.

"She won't be much trouble I can guarantee it!"

"Not much trouble? Kelly, she hates me, why should I?"

Kelly grabbed either side of my face and pulled me in for a long loving kiss and then said, "If you do this, tonight I will put on that little outfit you like and let you have your way with me, anything you want!"

"She can move into mine then!"

It was Rocket who had appeared in the doorway.

"Very funny Rocket, what do you want?"

"Let her move in you miserable sod."

"Yeah thanks mate, it looks like she probably will be doesn't it!"

Kelly leapt up on me and I had to catch and hold her as she wrapped her legs around my waist and kept kissing me. I'm still not sure it was worth it.

"You're the best!" She said before climbing down.

"Yeah Harry, you're the best!" Mocked Rocket.

"Get lost; I'll deal with you later!"

We started to make our way out when Kelly stopped and picked something up, it was a few bits of paper spilled out of a file which I thought I'd kept hidden away.

"By the way, what's all this?" Kelly asked picking it up. It was a load of legal jargon for a bit of land that had also been left to me, in London, Sands End area, out near the Imperial Wharf next to Chelsea Harbour. I didn't have a clue what I was supposed to do with it but was something that I needed to sort.

"Oh, that's a bit of paperwork from my lawyer. It's a bit of land I own apparently! My uncle's dad, is that my great uncle? Anyway, he bought it in the 40's and left it for my uncle, who in turn, left it for me and now it's mine."

"That's not it though is it Harry?" Rocket added with a smirk, "Tell her what its worth!"

"We don't know what it's worth Rocket."

"Well, maybe not but what has that developer offered you for it?"

"It doesn't matter; I don't know what to do with it. I might just keep it."

"What's the offer?" Kelly asked all intrigued.

"I can't remember, it says in that file somewhere."

"Can't remember?!" Rocket started laughing, "I can, and it was for four-million quid!"

"Four million pounds!?" Kelly screamed. "Four million pounds?! What's to think about? Sell it!"

"And put your mum in a home?"

"Very funny! Why didn't you tell me about this?"

"Well, would your opinion have changed of me if you knew I was worth millions?!"

"No!"

"Well you say that and I'll take your word for it because you didn't know about it. And for that small fact, I am eternally grateful as I know you're not just after my money!" I was joking but also being totally honest.

"I'm in shock!"

"DON'T tell ANYBODY okay?! No mum and definitely no Charley!"

"Okay, no problem."

"I mean it Kelly. Not a soul."

"Not a soul, zipped mouth."

"Promise me."

"Come on, you can trust me. I promise. On the lives of our future children!"

That was quite nice. I knew she loved me and I was never quite sure why, now she actually had a reason to I suppose, in a pessimistic view sort of a way.

"That's good; now let's get back to our party shall we?"

"Let's but I'm shaking!"

"We'll just tell people we had a quickie up here if anyone asks." I said as all three of us left the room and I switched off the light and closed the door.

"Speaking of quickies," Rocket pulled me aside as Kelly headed towards the stairs. "You got any rubbers? We've made up!"

"No rocket, I don't. And also, come here," he went on tip-toes and tilted his ear to my mouth as I continued, "and you don't fucking need them now do you?!"

TWENTY

After explaining to Rocket that I didn't actually mean anal, Kelly had already made it downstairs. I wanted to catch up with her just to make sure she would be keeping quiet. In my mind, nothing should change at all, but as they say, money is the root of all evil. I obviously trusted Kelly and didn't think anything would change there, or at least I hoped it wouldn't. But what worried me was Charley, what would she be like if she ever found out her sister was marrying a potential millionaire. It made me shudder. I couldn't get Kelly to sign a so-called pre-nup but could I somehow get something in there about not letting her crazy sister near it. Not that I harboured any ambition to kick the bucket before my time but it made you think about these things. I'd have to speak to my lawyer about everything anyway. Maybe I could even set up a trust fund for kids when we have them. Kelly didn't come across as a greedy wannabe millionaire so maybe she'd let it slide until she popped out a couple of chavs.

I was back downstairs and saw Kelly talking to a few of our friends and just gave her bum a little tap as I walked past, I liked doing that, it was after all, a good bum. I carried on past until I saw Iris still sitting there, with an almost finished cucumber. She was on her own as I noticed Charley was at the bar, again. Whether it was just to get more drink or to chat up Thor I wasn't sure, in fact, I didn't care. But this gave me chance to go and speak to *the virus* whilst she was on her own, no prompting from Charley or if she does put on a front, maybe it'll drop a bit now.

"How's the cucumber?" One of the strangest opening lines I think I've ever said.

"Nearly finished," as she popped the last bit in her mouth and continued, "nice wet one it was." At least that's what I assumed she said through the spit and green gob-full of mush.

"Oh good. Lovely. Can you get dry ones then?"

"You'd be surprised. Some real shockers out there."

"What's the secret then? Fresher the better?" What the fuck was I talking about? Who cared about cucumber moisture?!

"Not sure, just depends on what Charley brings back from Aldi. Sometimes they're good, sometimes they're not. But at 11p each who is complaining?"

Erm, you.

"I suppose you're right Iris. Anyway, about you moving in? That's fine with me; I mean us, Kelly and me. I'll come and get you on Monday if you like, give you a hand?"

"I was moving in anyway sunshine. Kelly already said and Charley has made arrangements."

"Well, you'd still need me to okay it wouldn't you Iris?" I said with an inverted smile.

"Nah."

"But you would." Even the fake smile was slipping.

"Not really, Kelly lives here; I'd just have come when you were at work."

"Yes, but I'd still need to okay it, that's what relationships are about."

"Whatever treacle, you tell yourself whatever."

I was getting lost for words. This ungrateful old bag in front of me with green shit stuck in her teeth was pissing me off.

"Well, we'll see how it goes shall we, just a week yeah." It wasn't a question.

"Do you think I want to stay here?!" She snapped back.

Yes Iris, I do. You ungrateful, wrinkly old beanbag.

"Do you not then?"

"Do I heck as like. I'll miss my bed and I'll miss my toilet."

As long as you don't *miss* my toilet, I thought. "Okay then, one week, nice and quick, and we'll get you back to your nice, newly painted house, where your toilet and bed will be waiting for you."

"Yep. One week." She said standing up, this conversation was apparently over. "Two at the most."

Why did I feel like a turkey that had just caught Bernard Matthews looking at him?

I tried to put the whole thing out of my mind for the rest of the night and have some fun, which at this stage needed a lot of alcohol. Which it got. It was actually a really good night, no more unnecessary dramas and I met Mandy properly. Who was really nice, in fact her and Rocket seemed to be getting on great, after their quick 'rekindling' procedure upstairs, he seemed really happy, whether it was the booze or the fact he was having a kid I wasn't sure, I'd suggest the former but he was definitely into this woman too, and to be fair, she was into him. Crazy times. She was a smiley person though, that I could tell, one of life's optimists which was something I always liked in people. I was sat next to her towards the end of the evening, well and truly at the struggling for words, but a wordsmith, stage of been drunk. Kelly was next to me, just leaning on me and Ethan and Claire had passed out on our table opposite us. What a sorry bunch we really were. Rocket though, he was still up on the dance floor cutting some rug and pulling some gravity-defining dance moves.

"He's got both feet hasn't he?" Mandy asked me; obviously she was sober as a judge.

"Erm, what's that now?" Trying to give myself time. I couldn't lie about it, she was having his baby, surely she'd find out soon. But I didn't want to tell her.

"Terry. I've known since the first time I met him that he wasn't an amputee, we can kind of tell."

"I don't want to get involved. It's a discussion for you and him before I start poking my beak in I'm afraid." What else could I say? It was a; *yes of course he's got both fucking feet* but also a; *but I'm not officially telling you that.*

"I know, I know. But it's not a big issue. I knew from the start but kind of liked the fact he was making such an effort," she said with me thinking that she may well be just as fucked up as him, "as you can imagine, blokes can't seem to get past the arm issue." I guess I saw in a strange way where she was coming from.

"Rocket is, erm, I mean Terry is a great guy, he really is. He will be 100% committed to you and this baby you know; there'll be no worries there. It just may take a while to see it."

"I don't think it will take that long. He proposed earlier!"

"What? You're kidding right?!" Who was I to judge though!

"Yeah, well no I'm not kidding, he did but he was very drunk so I said we'd talk about it in the morning. I'll let him bring it up."

Probably wise I thought and just nodded in agreement. He liked doing things off the cuff but this was out of the blue completely. He'd turned up here a single man; he's waking up in the morning engaged to a woman carrying his baby, what a night!

It was quiet for a minute as we both just watched Rocket dancing away on the dance floor, on his own. He really was what I'd call special. You could take that as you pleased. I couldn't help but keep looking at Mandy though, well, more like her missing arm. These types of things didn't bother me but what did always fascinate me was how the person coped. I'd spend hours grilling her if I didn't think it was rude or the fact she's probably been asked them a thousand times before. I had a few questions I'd ask when we got to know each other a bit better I decided. But not before she caught me looking at her and deep in thought.

"Do you want to touch it?" She asked me waving the stump my way. It made me jump I'm ashamed to say.

"Sorry, no, its fine thanks. I'm just intrigued by it, BY YOU sorry. I'm intrigued with how you cope and deal with it?

"Well, it's just normal to me, I lost it when I was a baby so never known any different. It was my parents that had to deal with the problems really. Even though I've always just been me."

"A baby? What happened? If you don't mind the question. I promise I won't ask another."

"It's fine, honestly. I get it. It's unusual but yeah, my mum had Rhesus negative blood type and when I was born they didn't know this and didn't give her the necessary injection, I came out and the was a problem, started in my hand and worked its way up my arm, they had to chop it off before it reached any further or any organs. So it was no arm or no life, so we see it as a reminder of how lucky I am."

As I said, she was a positive person, I'd be more about the fact the doctors fucked up but she was one of the good ones.

"So," I started, and thought it was time to test the humour pool, "when Rocket, I mean Terry, proposes properly, where does he put the ring?" It was a fair question right?

"I do have fingers over here," she said wiggling them at me, maybe I'd gone to early on the silly questioning.

"I *did* think that but wondered what the religious meaning of the left hand and finger etcetera meant." Trying to dig myself out of my drunken hole.

"It's a fair question I suppose but I'm sure when it comes around to it we'll figure something out."

"Yeah absolutely, sorry about the question."

"Honestly, no worries. Believe it or not, I'm used to getting questions. And abuse."

"Really, people can be terrible can't they, even in this day and age, with war heroes and all that, you think the world would be more realistic." I was babbling.

"Yeah but you'd be surprised, at least once a week somebody will say something to me, like clap or *you alright? Course you are, you haven't got a left*. Hilarious. Believe me, I've heard them all."

"Harry," It was Charley, she'd headed over our way, with the barman now that it had closed. "I'm taking him upstairs; I'd hang back if I was you."

"Brilliant."

"Great, see you in the morning. Night Handy, sorry, Mandy." And with that she was off.

"Sorry about her" was all I could say to Mandy, not that it was my place to apologise for her. I don't even know why I thought I should have to.

Mandy was fine about it, even laughed it off. As she said, she'd heard it all before. Rocket came back over after he'd finished dancing, which in itself was ten minutes after the music had stopped. We chatted for about half an hour in between them having epic bouts of tonsil tennis. She still didn't ask him outright about his foot but was definitely playing with him, asking about his dance moves and watching him squirm. I was definitely going to like her. I woke Kelly up to head upstairs, hoping Romeo and Juliet had finished their business. Most people had left but as we walked out the marquee, in the corner were two women I knew. One had her dress hitched up and knickers around her ankles squatting on a bucket, where she got the bucket I don't even know, it wasn't mine.

"You alright there Tandy?" I asked her on our way out of the tent.

"Oh hi Harry," came the slurry reply, "fine thanks. Just having a wee."

"Okay. You know there are two toilets in the house?"

"This is easier. Thanks though."

I looked at the woman stood next to her watching her and holding a couple of napkins.

"Lisa? You okay there?"

"Fine thanks, just waiting for her to finish so I can go next."

I couldn't even find a response and carried on to bed dragging Kelly along. She asked me in a sleepy-drunk tone;

"Who is that?"

"That's my bank manager."

TWENTY ONE

The next morning, although my head was a little fluffy, I dragged myself downstairs to check out the mess from the night before. In theory, this was Charley's deal so she should be clearing everything up or at least has it arranged but I wasn't holding my breath. On my way down the stairs, Charley was heading up them; I stopped at the bend in them to let her past. She was carrying two cups of either tea or coffee and was just wearing the shirt of the barman from the night before.

"I've got a team of people coming into to clean up in about forty-five minutes so you can just ignore the mess down there." She said not stopping.

"Nice shirt."

She stopped and looked down to realise what I was saying.

"Thanks, what was in it last night was better though."

"Nice. When you moving out did you say?"

"Tomorrow I will, probably just spend today in bed if you know what I mean?"

"Why not. Maybe I'll start renting my rooms out by the hour like a seedy American hotel?"

She just gave me a bit of a snarl and carried on to her room whilst saying "You'll miss me once I'm gone!"

"Like George Michael missed Andrew Ridgley maybe."

She stopped at her door and looked at the handle and the two cups of tea and nodded for me to walk over and open it up for her. As I headed over she said, with a laugh "you say that, but you'll have mum here next. I'll be seen as a breeze."

"As long as your mum doesn't bring barmen back to her room rattling headboards all night I think it'll be a step up."

I opened the door and let her in, I couldn't help but notice this naked man tied to the bed.

"Good luck mate." It was all I could say; I didn't want to add that I hope his balls stay intact.

Charley gave me a filthy look and told me to close the door and basically fuck off. As I closed the door I couldn't help but smile. That poor bloke won't know what has hit him. I walked across the landing as the next bedroom door opened and out came Rocket. Fucking hell, it is like a sleazy motel.

"What you doing here?!"

"Sorry mate, I couldn't get a cab and Mandy was randy if you get my meaning."

"Yes Rocket, I get your meaning, of course I get the very straight forwardness of your meaning. Just bring the sheets down when you leave."

"Okay mate," as he headed to the toilet, "you want to wash them straight away then."

"Wash them? I'm burning them."

I headed downstairs and the place was a mess, as expected. I'm so glad I didn't have to tackle it. I planned to make some tea and toast and take it up to Kelly but saw that Charley had used the last of the milk. And black tea is just a big no. I found some orange juice though and took her up with some jam on toast. Kelly was still asleep, she looked hungover despite being asleep but still I couldn't help but look at her. I was a lucky guy. She was the perfect woman for me, for anyone I suppose; I was just the lucky one. I was sat thinking what I could do to surprise her today, take her to the zoo or something 'coupley', when I suddenly remembered about her mum moving in tomorrow. My toast suddenly got lumpy in my throat and the orange was warm and had bits in. Kelly wasn't getting any treats today! Mind you, how long could I stay mad at her and wasn't sure, she'd definitely pulled a fast one here, I was sure of it, but did I actually care? I still had her, which was more important than having some old cobweb-head move in. Still, something in the back of my mind was telling me that I needed to start putting my foot down a bit, things like this, her mum, Charley moving in, planning our parties, it was snowballing and needed nipping in the bud, or butt as Kelly would say. Yes, today was the day I was changing, I was going to tell her when she woke up that her mum has only one week here, Charley is not coming back nor planning our wedding and that was that, no more Mr push-over. I noticed she was starting to wake up, I'd put her toast and orange down next to the bed and the smell must have started to hit her nose.

She started to sit up, despite obviously feeling really ropey, and smiled a huge smile;

"Morning handsome, is that my toast I can smell?" As she straightened up and got comfy with her back against the headboard, the duvet slipping down.

"Yep. Shall we go to the zoo today?!"

Okay, okay. I'm a pushover. But there were magnificent boobs staring at me!

We were up and out of the house before anyone saw us, thankfully. It was a right knocking shop there at the moment. All sorts of noises coming out of my spare rooms. We actually heard less strange noises when we were at the zoo.

It was a really fun day at the zoo though, great day to just stroll around, it wasn't particularly cold and the sun was bright. It was one of those days you really enjoyed with someone you loved; we chatted, laughed, moaned, ate, drank and kissed. We were like a cheesy advert, but I didn't care. I was planning on bringing up her mum situation again, I didn't want to ruin this perfect day but I had to get ready to say what I was thinking, but how to open up the conversation was a struggle. Luckily, I didn't have to.

"I just wanted to say," Kelly started "how bloody great you are."

"Thanks, I know." That got a shove.

"No, just with the whole Charley situation and now with mum, you are being so great about it. I know it's a lot to ask."

"Well, you know I want the house to feel as much yours as mine, so you can invite anyone you want to stay."

"You really mea......." She was in the middle of saying before I spoke a bit louder to carry on.

"Obviously, things like this need to be a discussion, same if say, Rocket needed a place to stay for a while, I'd speak to you, then offer him the spare room for a week or so. After speaking to you." I added again, just to make sure.

"I know, I get it. I *get* it. I'm just a bit impulsive like that. I'm sorry but I knew you would have said yes anyway so, you know."

She had me there I suppose, I would always be swayed by her and I knew it, worse still, she knew it. But this still didn't want this being a regular thing, but whom else was there for her to move in? So was it worth pushing the point?

"I probably would have but that's not the point. From now on, we discuss big decisions *before* offering our residence to people. Agreed?"

"Of course!" and apparently that was that.

We were near the apes and getting ready to head off to a pub for a bit a bit of dinner when I remembered that I always wanted a pet chimp;

"I always wanted one of these; I used to beg my mum and dad for one."

"Really? How old?"

"I wouldn't care. As long as it was healthy"

"Oh ha-ha, how old were *you!*"

"I don't know, six or seven I suppose, probably until I was, well, to be honest, I'd have one now."

"Why haven't you got one then?"

"I'm pretty sure it's not allowed. Anyway, I ended up having an imaginary orangutan called Morris, just like the one from that Clint Eastwood movie. Everyone thought I was weird at the time but me and Morris, we were great."

"Imaginary monkey?"

"Well, orangutan."

"What's the difference?"

"It doesn't really matter, what's important is that I was a little mental kid with an imaginary pet. Did you ever have any imaginary friends?"

We left the enclosure and started to make our way to the exit then look for some good pub grub, somewhere around Regent's Park or head into Camden, we're trendy like that you see.

"I didn't have any of my own imaginary friends," Kelly started, "I just played with Charley's."

I couldn't figure out quite how strange that comment was. This family I was about to inherit were all bonkers by the look of it!

TWENTY TWO

We got back home and saw Charley sat happily on the sofa with a tub of Ben and Jerry's.

"Shouldn't you be packing?" I asked before bothering to say hello, "big swap day tomorrow!"

"Why? Pointless moving my stuff back if I'm just going to painting the whole house."

Shit, that made sense. "Yeah but, surely you'll need a few essentials so you don't need to come back here?"

"Nah, I'll just bag a few bits up in the morning. I need to rest now." She said and gave Kelly an exhaled lip wobble whilst wafting her hand around her crotch.

"Oh yes, this ice cream for two is it? Where is the hunk?" Kelly asked. Hunk? Hang on.

"No no, you won't be seeing him again."

I was going to ask what she had done with the body but instead opted for a joking-not joking comment of; "or hearing him again let's hope'

"I can't help it if I get a fella off several times a night can I? And him me," she looked at Kelly and continued, "honestly Kel, it's like a punctured rugby ball down there, I'm ruined!"

"For fucksake! I can't believe I'm actually looking forward to your mum moving in tomorrow."

"Do you reckon her fanny is in a better state than mine then?!" She asked sitting up properly.

"What? I'm not having, erm, what?! I'm not having this conversation you freak."

She started laughing. "I love making you squirm!!"

I just shook my head and headed to the kitchen out of her sight. Kelly followed me in there as Charley carried on laughing before turning the tele up.

"Don't let her get to you." Kelly said putting her arms around my waist and pulling me in for a kiss.

"Get to me? She's fucking mental. Who brings up their mum's old fanny in a conversation? I think I threw up a little in my mouth."

"Ha-ha, it was a weird one that," Kelly said as she left me and filled the kettle, "but you had best just hope you don't see it. My mum won't wear clothes in bed and she will walk around the house if she can't sleep."

"Fuck right off!"

"She's old, it's effort to keep moving clothes up and down when you go to the toilet six or seven times a night."

"That's it. We will have a system in place. You will be up first and make sure she is up and FULLY dressed, then you release me from our bedroom. But only once its all clear and she has clothes on. No way am I running the risk of seeing that powdery old minge."

"Tea?"

"Did you hear me?"

"Yeah, sure, system. Got it. She's old so try and see it from her point of view. Tea?"

"I think the fact she is old just adds to the many reasons *I don't want to see my mother-in-law's vagina*!"

"Point taken. Tea?"

"I think I'll have a beer."

The morning was here and I'd actually slept really well, maybe because there wasn't any strange cowboy screams coming from the bedroom next door or *bedrooms* probably. It was hard to tell. My god I was sounding like a right old fart. But I had woken up in a decent mood, yes, a miserable old cucumber muncher was moving in but at least the barman muncher was moving out. I suppose it was a bit like finding two tenners and then losing a twenty pound note.

It was a Monday morning and I got ready and left for work. Kelly had taken the day off (she had a good boss it seemed) to help sort her mum and Charley out. I wasn't sure whether to head back at lunch to check up on what was happening under the disguise of actually offering to help or just wait until I'd finished later and just see how it was over the dinner table. As it happened I had to take somebody to Stansted airport around lunchtime so that made my mind up. Of course, the idea of jumping on a plane at Stansted and just sodding off to the Bahamas did cross my mind. If only Kelly wasn't so damn lovely! Bitch.

I phoned Kelly on my way back along the M11 to see how things were going, I was told everything was fine and everything was nearly sorted but I was needed when I got back to fit a toilet seat. I didn't even ask how the old one got broken but was sure I'd find out that little treasure over dinner. I had remained in a good mood all day though really. Why? Kelly. Whenever I thought about how shit this week was going to be with Iris the Virus (or Covid I decided I'd call her with my friends for code) was going to be, there was always Kelly. Had I pictured it differently? Sure. Would I change it? Abso-fucking-lutely. At the expense of my relationship? Not a chance.

The rest of the afternoon was pretty easy and I was pulling on my drive behind Kelly's car not long after 5pm. I should have kept on driving.

"Hello!?" I shouted as I walked through the door. Maybe just to make sure *Covid* wasn't walking round in her crusty buff.

"We're in the kitchen!" Was the shout back. From Charley!

As I started to walk that way Kelly came running downstairs, "Hi." And she gave me a kiss. "Did your afternoon go okay?"

"Hmm, so far. What's going on? You're fidgety."

"Who? Me? No, I'm good. Just missed you." And she kissed me again.

"Kelly?"

"Erm, yeah?"

"I'm not going through there to be ambushed again. What's happened?"

"Nothing much. Charley just needs to stay here a little longer."

"WHAT?!"

"My mums needs some proper work doing to it, nobody can go in there whilst it's been done. Underpinning or something."

"Underpinning? She's only supposed to be having the fucking bedroom painted."

"Well, Charley was painting it and she discovered cracks she could get her hand in, she called a builder and got moved out."

"All in one day?"

"So she says."

"And you knew nothing about this?"

"Not until she got back here around 3pm and filled me in. I swear."

This was not happening. "How about we go stay at the place we are getting married for the week, bit of a rehearsal for the big day?" I wasn't even close to joking.

"Don't be silly. This will be okay, I promise."

"Whatever. I'll be working a lot this week then."

"Come on, I've made dinner. Carbonara, it's good and then we'll all play scrabble tonight hey?"

"Scrabble? You're offering me scrabble? Charley can't even spell scrabble."

"It'll be fun."

I threw my coat on the end of the bannister and started to walk towards the now dreaded kitchen. I could picture Charley's smug face, probably sat on something that isn't a chair and I wasn't looking forward to it. Then I saw, propped in the corner, a grotty toilet seat. Not a new toilet seat but one that looked like it had survived many wars.

"What. The. Fuck. Is. That?" I asked pointing at something I'm sure Henry VIII had sat on.

Kelly was busy moving my coat from the bannister and hanging it up under the stairs. "Sorry, mum thinks it's untidy to leave coats hanging round. Erm, yeah, that's the seat that mum needs fitting to our loo."

"I'm not touching that with a shit-filled arse never mind with my hands to fit it. Do you have any idea how close your head gets to those things when you fit them? Fuck that. No way! What did you say about my coat?"

"I'll help you, we can wear gloves. Erm, yeah, coats live under the stairs now, on those hooks."

"What hooks?"

"Hooks I put up today to hang coats on. It makes perfect sense."

I honestly couldn't even be arsed to say anything. I would carry on putting my coat at the bottom of *my* stairs in *my* house, if people wanted to move it then that's up to them. Fucking bell-whiffs. I braced myself for my walk into the kitchen with a deep breath. Charley, as expected, was sat *on* the breakfast bar, Covid was sat at the table talking to her, a mostly-chewed cucumber on the table.

"Here he is! Now we are all together like a nice big family!" Charley said with in a huge *I fucked you* tone.

"Evening."

"Can you go put my toilet seat in? I've been pinching one in for about an hour." First thing her mum said. How far away was Stansted again? I honestly considered telling her to just get out, both of them. Offer to pay for them at the Premier Inn or whatever but I knew Kelly would kick off. Wrongly so in my eyes but I didn't want to upset her. Yet.

"So, how many grannies did you get to their hairdresser's today then O.A.P.MAN. Not all superheroes wear capes you see mum. Well, unless you're trying to perv over me in the bath at about three in the morning of course."

"What's that?" Iris enquired.

"Nothing Iris, where's this seat then?" I'd decided however disgusting this toilet seat idea was, it still beat the idea of talking to these two wankers. I told Kelly to carry on doing dinner whilst I went and sorted this, she asked if I was sure and as I intended to pour acid on my hands once I'd finished I told her it was best if she stayed downstairs.

I managed to fit it with surprising ease. It weighed an absolute tonne but all the holes lined up and it was done thank god. I washed my hands about four times and went to the bedroom to change, probably throw away the shirt; maybe work would give me a new one that fitted.

As I came out the bedroom, after taking my sweet time, I was in no rush to get back down there despite being starving, I thought I'd have a quick wee, walking to the bathroom trying to think if I was going to just piss with the seat down or try and lift it with a foot or something, I didn't realise that the light was on but the door wasn't locked so in a walked. Iris was sat on the loo, her dress was completely off for some reason and she was making an almighty groan and I heard the plop. I tried not throwing up absolutely everywhere as the noise was quickly followed by the smell. Luckily I managed to back out without her seeing me. You might wonder why she hadn't seen me. Well, she sits on the toilet to do her business, facing the cistern. The wrong way around. Like some sort of wrinkly kid on a carousel, hugging the head of the horse. It's an image I'll keep with me until my dying day. I stood in shock on the landing for a good minute or so before heading downstairs just thinking why on earth these fucking weirdo's that had invaded my home didn't know how to lock a fucking bathroom door!

TWENTY THREE

It was an awful dinner that night. The food was lovely but watching Iris eat spaghetti was not for the light-hearted. Slurping doesn't even begin to describe the noises coming out of that woman. Okay, maybe she is old and can't help it but the sheer glee on her face as she looked at me whilst doing it told me differently. And the conversation didn't help my queasiness. We were back on cameras and body-holes.

"So," Iris was saying, "I've been told I need another scan, front chute."

"Iris, do you mind if we don't talk about this at dinner time please? Not for my sake you understand, but you know, it must be a distressing for you having to think and talk about it?"

"Oh it doesn't bother me sunshine, I'm sure I must have told you before but can't feel a thing down there."

"Can't remember if I'm honest with that one Iris."

"Yep, dead as a dodo, not sure why."

"This is lovely food Kelly, I can get used to this." I said trying to divert conversation away from covid over there.

"You could probably throw a disposable camera up there with a photographer and I wouldn't know."

"How was your day anyway honey?" Come on Kelly, answer quickly!

"I'll need somebody to come in with me when I go through girls."

"Okay mum, we'll sort something, don't worry." Kelly finally spoke.

"Yeah and if we can't make it, I know a soon to be family member that drives a taxi. I'm sure he'll take you and come in and hold your hand." Charley piped in.

I just stuffed the last, huge mouthful of pasta in and just sort of gestured with my eyebrows.

"Sorry honey, yes my day was fine thanks. Back to work tomorrow, but Charley will be here to make sure mum is okay."

That's good to know, I'll be working from 4am until midnight for the next week or two I wanted to say, but instead I just finished my mouthful and said; "That's good. I'll clear the table and wash-up if everyone has finished?"

They all nodded and Kelly thanked me, the other two didn't.

"What are you doing with those leftovers?" Iris enquired.

"Erm, what leftovers, Kelly served it all up."

"Yeah, but I've left some and so have these two."

"That's not left-overs Iris, that's more like, well, scraps."

"Nonsense! Scrape them together in a bowl and I'll eat them at some point."

"Some point when? I don't think pasta keeps too well. I'll stick it in the food bin."

"You will do no such thing! But them in a plastic tub and stick it in the freezer; I've brought tubs with me, just label what it is."

"You've brought tubs?"

"Mum likes to keep every little bit of food. Your freezer will be full of bread by the weekend." Charley decided to add.

"Great. Nobody likes wasting food hey Iris. I think it's a great idea." I was trying a different approach to try and throw Charley. "I'll put this stubby end of garlic bread in there too."

"Don't be silly! That will never be the same again after freezing; it'll be like a bloody weapon. Take my jaw off I'd bet if I tried chewing that after a month in your freezer."

"Oh right, no problem. I just need to tak…. Hang on, a month in my freezer? Why would that possibly be relevant to you?"

"Well, you just don't know about this underpinning do you?" Charley said with glee.

"I know nothing about underpinning. I do, however, know about my own house and guest limitations."

"Dessert anyone?" Kelly was up trying to divert the conversation. Or defuse it maybe.

"Well," I said taking the hint, "why don't we leave this discussion for another day."

"Good idea," Kelly said heading to the kitchen, "we'll talk more about it next week together."

"Or," I said a bit more loudly than I planned, "we could pencil it in for tomorrow, proper chat about it and maybe putting some final dates on things, what do you think?"

"If we can, we will." Iris said exhaling, but then did add, "thanks' for putting us up. I know it's a lot to ask."

Where did that come from!? I thanked her for saying it and said it wasn't a problem and she was always welcome, just trying to be polite back. Had I just fallen into a trap? Had I just made what will turn out to be a big mistake?!

Later that night I got out of the shower, Kelly was in the bathroom too as we now had to cut down our time in there I suppose, It was a four bedroom house and although there was a downstairs toilet there was no en-suite, it had never been an issue before. Could I get one fitted this week?! Kelly had finished her shower and was, I don't know, taking her face off? Or at least applying some sort of cream as I got out of the shower. I hadn't brought anything up about the current living situation. Why bother?

We both started brushing our teeth, still without really saying anything of interest, we'd mainly been talking about what we would be doing tomorrow, work, after work, dinner blah blah, the sexy exciting times of this relationship were dying fast! To be fair, it was a bit of a killer having your mother-in-law down the hall when you're going at it. Plus I was getting vibe off Kelly tonight that it was definitely a straight to sleep situation.

I tipped my head forward to spit out my last bit of toothpaste as Kelly finished gargling her mouthwash. Now, she leans right into the sink to do the politest spitting you could possibly do, I hadn't noticed she was leaning right into the sink getting rid of said mouthwash when I dropped my unwanted toothpaste out from a much higher height, straight onto the back of her very recently washed hair. She stopped still; I stopped too, could I laugh, should I laugh? I wanted to but just stood there holding my brush like I'd turned up at a knife fight with a terrible weapon, not knowing what to do. Kelly slowly lifted her head and looked at me.

"Sorry about that." I said still will too much froth around my mouth. "Minty hair? Could be the future?"

Yep definitely not a laughing matter, women take slightly longer over their hair then men it would seem. She walked past me, dropped her dressing gown and got into the shower, again. Oh yes, sex was certainly off the table tonight.

The next morning I was awake around 6am and thought that I should just lay in bed until I'd heard the different footsteps in and out of the bathroom and work could wait, but as I hadn't heard anything in the ten minutes I'd been awake I thought I might brave it and go to the bathroom, because basically, I really needed to. But, thinking about it, I could be ready, eaten breakfast and get out the door this morning before having to see anyone, I could even leave Kelly a little note like they do in the movies with an orange juice and a rose, claiming I had an early start and I didn't want to wake her. Hey, maybe I could do this for two weeks. Mind you, my favourite part of the day was watching this woman wake up or waking up to her myself but under the current circumstances I could go a few days of not doing it. After all, we'd have all our lives together for me to enjoy that.

I decided my bladder didn't deserve the torture and made a break for the bathroom. I think that I heard movement around 3 this morning, which by the deep grizzle; I assumed it was Iris going for one of her naked pisses. I hadn't heard anything since so I was going for it. I got up put a pair of shorts on, my shorts, definitely, and dug out a t-shirt. I'd come back to get dressed for the day after I was done weeing and brushing my teeth. I thought again about last night and spitting on Kelly's head, it made me chuckle, she'll find it funny too eventually I was sure of it. I was slowly opening the bedroom door and saw it was a clear run to the bathroom and off I went, I don't want to over hype it but it felt like I was going over the top of the trenches in World War One. My head was down, took a deep breath and made the dash for it and I was pretty much there with no doors along the way opening or floor boards creaking on my journey, the adrenaline got me through it!

Once I was in the bathroom I double-checked, hell, triple-checked nobody was in there and turned and closed the door and locked it. I let my head rest against the door and I let out a big breath. I must have been holding it all that time, but hey, I'd made it.

I turned back around to face the bathroom and in my hurry to check for actual people on my entry and hadn't noticed the blue. Blue absolutely everywhere, blue stains on three of my formerly white towels, the sink was awash with blue, the floor had blue splodges over it, footprints maybe and even the taps were riddled with this strange blue residue. What the fuck was it? I examined a few bits but just didn't have a clue. Then there was a knock on the door, luckily it was Kelly. I opened the door;

"Look at this!" No good morning, which I should have done but I was not in the mood for pleasant words.

Kelly walked in and looked as bemused as me.

"What th...?"

"Haven't got a clue." Was all I could muster. There was a little cellophane wrapper on the floor which Kelly picked up.

"Oh god, no." She said and headed out of the bathroom.

"What? What is it?"

"Mum!" Kelly was banging on her mums door. "Mum, you awake?!" Bloody should be now I thought.

There was a bit of a thud on the floor and I heard the shuffling of feet.

"Hang on Love, I'm coming, what is it?"

The bedroom door opened, after what felt like an hour and stood there, was a wrinkly naked body which in itself would make me instantly turn away but the fact she was mostly covered in blue smears with an almost completely blue face made me keep looking.

"Mum, what the... what the hell has happened?!" She looked past her into her room and saw all her bed sheets were covered in bits of blue. "Jesus Christ! What has bloody happened?!"

I was hoping for hypothermia but it wasn't that.

"What is it love, what you going on about?"

"Mum, can you put your gown on or something please. Look! What... Why is blue absolutely everywhere? Is it because of this?" Kelly asked holding up the wrapper.

Thankfully her mum had put her dressing gown on and started to register what was going on.

"Is that the soap I opened last night?"

"Soap? What soap? I asked, now brave enough to come closer and stick my head into the room. Fuck me. It looked like the cast of Avatar had had an orgy in there.

"In the middle of the night I realised I hadn't washed before I went to bed, probably because of the congestion in the bathroom," she looked at me and I was a little dig there for some reason for only having one bathroom, or maybe that Kelly had to have two showers last night? "So I woke up and thought I'd best go give myself a body-wash. You know I don't do showers."

"Go on." Kelly urged.

"Well, that's about it love. I got to the bathroom, I didn't want to put a light on in case I woke you or Charley up (not me I noticed) so I just did it in the dark, I've done it a hundred times before so it wasn't a problem. Except I couldn't find the soap at first but then I found it in the cupboard underneath you know? I couldn't find the bar of Imperial Leather that I brought but I did find one of those little free soaps you get from hotels that we all save, well, for reasons such as this I suppose, anyway, I unwrapped it and had my wash, dried myself and came back to bed. Why? What is the problem? The soaps weren't being saved for something important were they?"

"No mum." Kelly said, "we don't have bars of soap here, it's the squirty stuff on the top of the sink in there, that's the soap we use, in fact, most people use these days. No, what you opened and used mum was a toilet cleaning block that you drop in the cistern."

"Bloo." I felt the need to add.

Her mum looked at us like we'd asked her to multiply 753,464 by 432,543. She slowly looked around and took in the amount of blue, or bloo, everywhere before looking at her own hands and looking back at me.

"Oh." Was all she could muster.

"It is a bit of an '*oh*' this one Iris isn't it?"

"I thought it was tough to unwrap but those little soaps are generally. And I thought it was a bit of a strong smell."

No shit was pretty much all I was thinking before she carried on;

"Well, why are they kept in the bathroom?"

"Erm, that's where the toilet is," I hit back.

"Bloody stupid if you ask me."

"Shall I maybe keep them in the shed then? Just pop down to the bottom of the garden when I notice after a wee that we need another one? You know, just in case somebody in the middle of the night decides to turn themselves citrus smelling smurf?"

"Well, somewhere better than under the sink is all I'm saying."

"Crazy place that, like, next to the bleach and toilet duck isn't it?" I was still closer to laughing, looking at this blue wrinkly face snarling back at me but I was not going to take the blame for this one. "And how and why have you used *three* towels?!"

"I always use three. One for my face, one for my top half and one for my bottom half."

I suddenly remembered the blue smears up her thighs heading inwards. Oh God. I was definitely going to start keeping my own towels in the bedroom as it seemed Iris would make any towel a fanny towel before just putting it back.

The other bedroom door opened and Charley was out on the landing next to me as Kelly was starting to sort their mum out and gathering the ruined towels.

"What the hell happened here?!"

"You'd best ask Sonic the Hedgehog's grandma here. I'm brushing my teeth and going to work away from this loony bin."

"What about breakfast?" Kelly asked.

"I'll get something on my way, it's too early for me this."

I brushed my teeth, got dressed and left for work, I quickly pulled Kelly aside and we both laughed about it. I guess I did feel a bit sorry for Iris here; I just keep picturing her face, luckily not the rest of her, smothered in bloo.

I was in my taxi and pulling out of the drive when unbelievably the first song came on the radio. Yep, it was by Blue. I laughed out loud and went to find breakfast.

TWENTY FOUR

It was a couple of days before Christmas, I was resigned to the fact I would have houseguests over this period but if I was being completely honest, it hadn't been as bad as I was expecting. They were still rude to me at every opportunity but as Kelly advised, I'd just ignore it and keep myself to myself as much as possible, which is exactly what I did. To get through the idea of Christmas and especially Christmas Day and dinner I'd invited Ethan, Claire, Rocket and Mandy. I hadn't seen any of them in the last week or so, in fact since the party. I'd obviously spoken to them by text but not met up for a good catch-up yet. Christmas seemed as good a time as any so they agreed and that would help me through what was sure to be a struggling day.

It was now Christmas Day and the others were due around about 1pm. The morning had been pretty miserable. It started well enough, with Kelly deciding Christmas morning should start with shag, and I wasn't going to argue. We swapped presents soon after that. We'd agreed not to go overboard because of our wedding, along with hen and stag do's, our birthdays and so on. Of course I completely ignored that and bought her a car. Well, it was a bit of a sneaky one as I was thinking about getting a car for myself for a while so I thought if I bought this and gave it to her as a present, it would save me trawling around women's shops looking for stuff and I could use it instead of always using the taxi. The taxi was a normal car, a Skoda, not a black cab but even so, you got bored of always being in it.

Anyway, Kelly opened up her present which was a box with a car key in it and screamed with delight. She did need a new car desperately, mind you, if it wasn't for her old banger we'd never have met as I reminded her as she was asking about how to get rid of it. The car I'd managed to get Rocket to drop off late last night, he still had one of the keys which I reminded myself to grab off him later, because he would just use it when he wanted otherwise.

I told Kelly to look out the window and sure enough at the end of the drive was a sparkling new orange BMW M3. I didn't like doing things by halves. And a woman that turned heads like her needed a car that also turned heads. Plus I was a boy racer at heart and liked a bit of a pose! I'd also had a meeting with my solicitor earlier that week about the land I owned, apparently a developer had gone up to a five million pound offer now, I knew I was going to sell it, hence the extravagance on the car and the fact we'd go all in for this wedding. No chicken option on the menu, we want quail eggs and oyster froth or whatever. But I was told not to sell yet. My solicitor advised me to hold off for a few more months, maybe another year; he thought I could get up to six, if not seven by then. I was in no rush nor need to sell it yet so I agreed. But my savings would be taking a big hit, but I didn't care. I wanted this to be a year to remember.

Anyway, after the excitement of the sex, the new car and erm, my new jumper it went downhill a lot quicker than I went downstairs. We gave Iris and Charley their presents, which Kelly picked and they were delighted. Charley got a new dress which looked like it would only fit a five year old but once she tried it on I realised it did actually fit, in fact, it fitted very well. Such a waste of a body, her being absolutely mental n'all. Her mum got and electronic hair remover, she'd asked for it apparently and it made me dread to think exactly where it was going to put to use.

Kelly then received her presents from them and she did pretty well, nice perfume and some shoes. Oh and a magic tree air freshener from Charley as she knew about the car, knew and also asked to be put on the insurance. 'I'd rather put Stevie Wonder on it' I think was my response.

I was handed my present which turned out to be a rectal thermometer, I have no idea why but Charley and Iris thought it was hilarious. I didn't get it, nor did Kelly but I didn't mind. What made my morning worse was what came just after that, as I was in the kitchen prepping for what is generally a stressful dinner, which I enjoyed doing so I wasn't complaining. Plus I had Kelly's help and had told the other two to stay out of the way.

But I was just sorting the roast potatoes out, all nicely laid out in a roasting tin, they'd been part-boiled, shaken so they had fluffy edges, smothered in goose fat and a little bit of rosemary added and were now ready to go in the oven. But it was then I heard from around the corner Kelly saying; *No, not today.*

"Not today, what?" I asked, walking out wiping my hands on a tea towel that was over my shoulder. My 'naked woman' apron well and truly been worn with pride.

"Oh nothing that can't wait." Kelly replied and went to walk into the kitchen past me. Charley stayed still and said;

"Well I'll tell him."

"No you won't!" Kelly stopped and headed back to Charley.

"Tell me what?" I knew I wasn't going to like it but it couldn't be left like this.

There was a moments silence before Kelly exhaled. She went to say something but nothing would come out.

"Kelly? What is it?" I asked again.

"I can't. Not today."

"I'll bloody tell him!" Charley said, again.

"You won't *tell* him anything. You can ask him though."

"Potato potarto. We have news about our house."

Oh God. "Really? All good I hope?" I said in sheer ignorant hope.

"Yeah, no not really. We got a letter yesterday. It's been condoned."

"Condoned?"

"Yeah, we can't go back to it."

97

"Do you mean condemned?"

"That's what I said."

"What do you mean, why has it?" I was genuinely perplexed.

"Well, it basically needs knocking down." Kelly added.

I gulped. Visibly. "That is bad news isn't it. What you going to do then?"

"Stay here bro!" Charley said, hit the top of my arm and headed into the living room.

I looked at Kelly.

"I swear," she started, "first week of January I'm out there looking at flats for them."

I didn't say anything, I just walked back into the kitchen and the first thing I saw was the potatoes. The only thought I had was that I wouldn't actually be able to eat them now at dinner. They were my favourite part normally. Why couldn't I have got this bombshell whilst I was doing the sprouts?!

I finished sorting the dinner in silence. I couldn't shake my shitty mood, and rightly so I thought. I couldn't even bring myself to cheer up when Kelly came in to cheer me up and give me kisses. After all, this was her fault. I knew I would be okay soon with her, I couldn't stay angry at her, she was only doing what she thought was right for her family, but I did think it was without consideration for me or my feelings, again. It was a strange position, for both of us. The fact she was in such a difficult position was the only way I was letting myself even come close to excepting this.

On one hand I was angry at not only the fact I had to live with these two absolute turds, nor that they didn't even seem remotely grateful, but the fact Kelly, despite our previous chats, made these decisions on her own, albeit probably with massive guilt tripping by the wicked witches of the east and west. But when I tried to think reasonably about it I could see that Kelly was in a real tricky situation, I wanted this house to feel like hers, it was a big house with the room so why wouldn't you help your family out when they're in such a jam. So I decided that, again, I'd take the hit, for her. I think the thing that got to me was how bloody twatty they both were towards me.

Maybe I'll have to get on top of that. Charley would probably just laugh in my face but maybe I could get through to covid, I mean she had already sort of said thank you.

Anyway, the next time Kelly came into the kitchen all sullen, I had a chat with her and explained my issues which, as expected, she fully understood. She said she'd have a word with them to be more appreciative but I had a feeling it might fall on deaf ears. Charley would probably just tell me to grow some balls. Or maybe chop them off.

The others were just arriving so at least now I could drink!

Ethan and Claire were first through the door; Rocket close behind with Mandy, who had driven. Something that Rocket said is pretty scary at first but she was a better driver than him. He told me this after I'd arranged for him to deliver Kelly's expensive new car.

I couldn't be happier to see them, for a couple of reasons, support against this pair of morons that were basically squatting at my house and also that they were carrying enough booze for a pirate ship. Kelly took their coats, and put them under the stairs, obviously. Rocket and Ethan followed me to the kitchen with the booze and we sorted drinks for everyone.

We said happy Christmas and chinked our bucks' fizz glasses together. It was actually pretty civil and quite nice.

"Surprised you two aren't spending today with your mum and dad?" It was Charley saying it to Ethan and Claire.

"They don't really know each other that well, yet. Maybe once we are married we'll have all four around for Christmas dinner." Claire said with a smile. I saw Ethan take a bigger mouthful of his drink when the 'M' word got mentioned.

"Oh right, four? I didn't say mums and dads," Charley said with a smirk exaggerating the S on both words. "Isn't there only *two* parents in this set up."

"What do you mean?" Claire didn't let her smile slip.

"Well, aren't you brother and sister?"

Luckily it fell down dead. Nobody laughed or even responded. Well, until Iris asked what she meant.

"Nothing mum," Kelly got in before Charley, "Ethan's sister goes out with Claire's brother, and Charley is just trying, and failing, to be funny."

"It is a bit weird though isn't it mum?"

"Wouldn't have happened in my day that's for sure."

"Whatever Iris, incest was rife in medieval times." I wasn't letting these two wind anybody up other than me today. And it brought a couple of laughs.

"People in Roman times did it to get true-blooded children." It was Rocket chipping in kind of missing the point. "Like in Gladiator." This is how he got most of his knowledge, films.

"But it doesn't happen that much these days does it?" Mandy said.

"Can I just add," Ethan responded, "this isn't incest."

"There is no blood link, I met Ethan a few years back and then about a year later my brother got together with Ethan's sister. We were all friends and in the same social circle because of us two getting together. I don't get the problem?"

"That's right," Kelly this time, "to be honest, I'm surprised it doesn't happen more often."

"Yeah that's right," I added, "maybe Charley; I'll introduce you to my brother. He looks a bit like Zac Efron."

"Whatever, if he's anything like you he'd be more like Zac Dingle."

"No seriously Charley, he does look like Zac Efron." Claire and Ethan both said and nodded.

"Really? Why the hell haven't I met him yet?! Where is he today?"

Everyone started laughing, well except for Iris and Charley.

"What?" Charley was bemused.

"I haven't got a brother. But you just proved our point. You would jump on him despite your sister going out with his brother!"

More laughing.

"Whatever you pack of bastards. I would if he looked like Zac Efron. Anyone would. I just wouldn't bother if he looked like that sorry excuse for a man." She said pointing at Ethan then necking her drink and stomping off to the kitchen.

We all smirked a bit and the Christmas day fun was well and truly underway.

TWENTY FIVE

Charley didn't want to be on the end of any jokes, never mind right at the start of the day and she was giving it back both barrels. Mandy was getting it, but she brushed all the comments off as I'm sure she'd heard them all before. Ethan couldn't care less what she said to him and even Claire was even laughing it off or completely ignoring her. Kelly and to be fair, Iris, had to keep warning her throughout dinner. I just kept eating and made sure everyone, except Charley, had their glasses filled. It was Rocket that finally bit though.

"So this poor baby you two are having? Are you sure it's fair to it?" She said, we had finished dessert by now and were just contemplating what to do. Chill out or play games.

"Why wouldn't it be fair?" Rocket replied as I took the dishes into the kitchen with Kelly.

"Well, you know. Look at the pair of you."

"What does that mean then?" Rocket was starting to snarl a bit. I think he was ready to defend Mandy after a couple of earlier digs he let go.

"Nothing. Hey, at least you've already got the *dad-bod* sorted. Twenty years early but its there."

"Don't listen baby," Mandy said whilst glaring back at Charley, "I like your body."

"You would, its whole."

"That's it!" Rocket stood up and started pointing at Charley. "Why don't you do us all a massive favour and just fuck off?!"

"Whatever little man, you and the one-armed bandit will be out of here before me. This is my house!"

I was back out of the kitchen and about to put her right about that when I saw Mandy pick up a massive handful of trifle that was still on the table and launch it at her face. And absolutely cover it. It was a great shot.

Charley didn't know how to react, she was in shock, she looked at Iris who was trying not to laugh and then at Kelly who after the initial shock started laughing loudly.

"What the fuck have you done bitch?!"

"Not bad for someone with one arm hey?"

Charley had no response.

"I don't think she can hear you baby," Rocket said grabbing Mandy into a hug. "Maybe she's a trifle deaf?"

It was a terrible joke but made us laugh more. Charley stood up and finally wiped her face before storming out telling us this wasn't over. We didn't care as it was so good seeing her in such a state. I was just hoping the revenge wouldn't be too extreme. Because it would definitely be coming.

The rest of Christmas day went well. Lots of alcohol, lots of talking and lots of fun. We played games and even Iris seemed to enjoy herself, well, in between the snarls and digs at me, and now Rocket too.

Mind you, Rocket didn't care, he was struggling to live down playing 'Ora' in the game of scrabble we had instead of 'Aura'. He argued it to death until he finally realised the Ora as in Rita, isn't the same spelling as the one needed for scrabble. Iris actually won that game; she had some serious luck at games it turned out. She managed to get the word *squeeze* in on a triple word square. We were done! I had a Y but I wasn't allowed squeezy, which was annoying because I'm pretty sure I also had throughout the game the letters to make the words easy, peasy and lemon. Still never mind, we were well onto the Cointreau's and Disaronno's of the world by then.

Charley had stayed upstairs not willing to come back down. Sulking I guess, or maybe plotting? I pictured her room; I mean my spare room, having elaborate drawings of revenge ideas a bit like Kevin McAllister in the Home Alone films. It was about 8pm when she finally came down but went straight out of the front door, not even glancing our way. We didn't know where she went but she was back around 10pm and came in holding a wing-mirror.

"I know I was out of order earlier," she began as she actually addressed the room, a pretty drunk room at this point, Iris was asleep in a chair and Mandy was sober but everyone else was in that silly drunk stage. "I shouldn't have said those things and I apologise, but I think somebody just *accidently* knocked your wing-mirror off Mandy I'm afraid. I just found it on the floor, I'm really sorry, but it was parked sticking out a little."

"Aren't all wing-mirrors sticking out? That's the point." Claire pointed out. All of us knowing full-well that Charley had snapped it off.

"Not the wing-mirror," Charley snapped a little, "the car. It wasn't parked very well, understandably I guess."

Mandy got up and approached Charley. What was going to happen we didn't know but the air felt like it had been sucked out of the room. Mandy was nice but Charley would wipe the floor with her if she tried anything here. As she approached she just put her hand out and nodded for Charley to put the mirror in her hand. No words.

The mirror was placed in her hand before anything was said, I was wondering if Mandy was going to hit her with it!

"That is strange." Mandy said.

"Not really, must be tough to get a car parked straight, even with power steering hey?"

"Not that, that's not that strange, it is tough to park sometimes. But what is strange is that my car has colour-coordinated wing mirrors."

"So do most cars these days, makes it really expensive to get put back on I suppose. So annoying. Christmas Day too." Charley said starting to take her coat off.

"Yeah, but my mirrors are at least matching the colour of my car…. This isn't my mirror."

"What?" Charley said her face dropping.

"This," Mandy said handing it back to her, "it isn't mine. My car is a lighter blue than this."

Rocket was out of the door and we all followed. Except for Iris that was well and truly asleep and snoring her head off.

Rocket walked past next doors house, the house on the right, and to a blue car with two mirrors still happily attached. "Both still on!" He shouted back a bit unnecessarily.

"Why did you park all the way over there?" Charley asked.

"Couldn't get any closer, there was a car there where there's now a gap, just behind that car there," pointing to the house to the left of mine, "the dark blue one, similar to mine, both VW Golfs but that one has a missing mirror."

"Shit," I said "that's Chapman's car."

Charley was looking around knowing she'd made a right tit out of herself again.

"What do you mean? Who is Chapman?" She asked.

"Chapman lives over there. And he is nuts! He is going to freak out. Luckily he has CCTV outside his house and pointing down the road so hopefully he'll be able to get a number plate of the car that did it. Or maybe the face of the culprit." I looked towards Charley, "Blimey though, you seriously wouldn't want to get on the wrong side of him, I heard a rumour once that out on a walk in Eastern Europe he got cornered by a wolf... and just punched it. Knocked it clean out if you please."

Charley handed me the mirror and ran back inside. Another victory I thought! Of course there was no Chapman but it didn't hurt to let her sweat a bit. Plus the owner of this damaged car didn't deserve it so maybe it was time to get some money out of her too. Oh yes, this was going to be fun, I just had to find the biggest bloke I know to pretend to be this angry neighbour and also figure out a way of paying Tony, the mild mannered brother of Sophie, my elderly next door neighbour, who must have been visiting for Christmas, the money for his mirror.

TWENTY SIX

In the New Year we started getting excited about our wedding. The plans were well on their way, as were the stag and hen dos. Yes, I was going to Blackpool. That was still a few months away, plenty of time to continue winding Charley up about the wing mirror. Or so I thought.

I got the biggest bloke I knew from down the pub to pretend to be the angry owner of this car, Chapman. I wasn't there when he came round in between Christmas and New Year to say he saw her on CCTV doing it and wanted paying but somehow Big Dan, the bloke I'd offered a few pints to for doing this, got caught up by the charms of Charley.

Now he was a big scary bloke but Charley had him wrapped around her little finger within hours. So much so, big Dan even paid Tony, the owner of the damaged car, out of his own pocket. What Charley had said to or even offered him I dread to think but she had beaten me here. Worst of all, she knew what I'd done and tensions in my own home were really stretched.

"I told you it wouldn't work." Kelly said to me as we climbed into bed one night. The night before New Year's Eve it was.

"No you didn't! You said it will teach her a lesson."

"Listen, you can't try and beat Charley at her own kind of games. And sending a bloke like Dan? Come on? She was always winning him over; little rub of the leg, letting him see the little looks she'd sneak at him, maybe even a well angled mirror when she's changing her top near him. She knows them all. Men become putty in her hands."

"You seem to know a lot about this?"

"I've known Charley all my life. She's a pro."

"Quite literally it would seem."

"Did I ever tell you about an ex-boyfriend of hers, called Smiffy?"

"Smiffy? With two f's?"

"Yeah, well that's what everyone called him. Anyway, she was with him for about six months, I don't know, she was about 20-21 I suppose. We thought it was pretty serious, Smiffy certainly did, because he thought, or maybe he was told she was playing around behind his back."

"Charley? As if!" I said with the biggest amount of sarcasm I could muster.

"Believe it or not, she actually wasn't. I don't think she ever has actually. She's very committed."

"She should be bloody committed I know that much."

"Behave, so, this Smiffy character decided to hire a private investigator, you know, to follow her around and keep tabs on her."

"That's a bit creepy."

"Isn't it? Touch insecure maybe Smiffy was, mind you, Charley was hot looking girl back then, still is of course, but a real head turner back then and she knew it. Still does."

"So, what happened?" I was actually sitting up waiting.

"Well, Charley got wind of this and she wasn't happy so she got him back."

"Is Smiffy still alive?"

"She left him alone yes. What she did got to him far better than any physical pain. She started shagging the P.I."

"What?! The private investigator he had hired?"

"The very same, made sure Smiffy found out about it in front of all his mates too. Poor bloke was never the same again."

"Jesus. I reckon I'll make-piece with her tomorrow. I'll get Rocket to do the same before she does something to ruin us!"

"Probably a smart move. And maybe get her involved in our wedding plans some more next week."

"Okay, that should smooth things over, good idea." We kissed each other goodnight, we were off out for New Year's Eve tomorrow, it would be a heavy one down at the local, so we were having a sensible early night. As I lay there trying to go to sleep for the next hour or so I couldn't switch my brain off. Was Charley that dangerous or was she just looking to be liked? But more importantly, I'd somehow been conned into actually wanting and asking Charley to take an active role in probably the most important year of my life. Charley was nuts and probably dangerous, but Kelly, I was beginning to realise, was a little bit of a cunning fox.

New Year's Eve came and went without much bother or excitement. I loved seeing the New Year in with Kelly, for that reason it will always be up there with a favourite of mine, but it was a pretty dull affair other than that. Mandy was a bit under the weather, so Rocket went home with her not long after 8pm, he had a cobb on about it;

"I've got to go." He said snatching their coats of the hooks.

"Everything okay?" Kelly and Claire both asked. After Ethan had asked if he needed help reaching the hooks. That didn't go down too well though the mood he was in.

"Bloody women and women's problems." He was muttering.

"Responsibilities now mate you see." I teased.

"Fuck that. I'm missing out on a New Year's Eve piss-up because she is on the rag."

We all looked at each other.

"Erm, she can't be Terry," Kelly stated what we thought was the obvious.

"What? Why not? You've seen how moody she has been tonight."

"She's pregnant Terry! Her hormones will be all over the shop, you need to be supportive"

"Shitting hell. For how long? She pissed me off this morning being sick loads. Put me right of my breakfast."

I hoped that Mandy couldn't hear any of this, luckily she was by the door waiting for him and her coat after already saying goodbye to us, and she'd already told us that morning sickness was kicking her arse.

"You'll need to be supportive for, hmm," Claire started, "about the next twenty years maybe?!"

Rocket just slumped his shoulders and headed towards Mandy and the door.

"Happy New Year mate," Ethan yelled, "she's a lucky lady, make sure you tell her that." We all had a little giggle as he sulked off murmuring something along the lines of that he will.

Apart from that little bit of drama it was a quiet night, no talk or sign of Charley, who was staying in with Iris. We were actually home by 1am, I did plan to see the New Year in with a bang but that was scuppered when we got through the door and Charley was up, and looked kind of sad.

She said how horrible she had been and said she was going to change; in fact, it was her New Year's resolution apparently. Where this was coming from I wasn't sure but I was happy to hear it. Maybe Iris had a word with her tonight, I spent most of the evening thinking they'd be here hatching plans but it seemed like that the exact opposite was happening. We in turn returned the affection in the moment I suppose you could say and asked her to be a big part of the wedding plans, it had been mentioned before but I think we all knew I'd be planning a way out of it, so hearing it from me meant she was happy and said she would be honoured and promised not to mess it up.

I still got to see the New Year in with a bang, an exceptional one as it goes, maybe because a lot of weight seemed to have been lifted off Kelly's shoulders. Yes, I'd gone from looking forward to this coming year enormously to dreading most of it, back to excited.

Of course, this didn't last all that long.

TWENTY SEVEN

The first couple of days went well. We started planning certain details and finalising things with photographers, fancy cars, florists and what have you and Charley was doing her bit. She'd already put a lot into it with Kelly but was starting to get into it more now she'd been asked by me. It seemed a while away the wedding but things needed sorting now. And Charley was planning the hen party, and I was a bit jealous of her excitement and effort she was putting into it. Ethan had sort of been pushed aside for mine by Rocket, hence Blackpool, but neither were really invested. Train, drink, sleep, drink, strippers, drink, sleep, train, was just about the gist of it. *'Minimal effort'* was the quote by both of them as if it was a good thing. Who knew, maybe it was.

It started going wrong around mid-February. Iris and Charley were still at mine, each week was their last week apparently, so much so I gave up asking. We were getting on fine so it didn't seem that big of a deal, which surprised even me. But I got home on this day to be told they couldn't get anywhere else to live together, at all. Iris had no money after always being in council houses and Charley wasn't working. No landlord would touch them, or at least no landlords that had decent houses. They were offered absolute dumps in dodgy areas but Kelly, rightly so, would say no way.

I had a feeling this arrangement would last longer than they originally suggested but this was months now, I'd given them the deadline of Easter off the back of this news. I thought that was reasonable but it turned Charley and Iris back into their old selves.

We weren't in a position to help, all our money was going into the wedding. The question that was burning Kelly finally came out after this bombshell had been dropped. She couldn't help it and asked me for a word upstairs. There was a time not so long ago that if Kelly was telling me to get upstairs I'd run up with her throwing clothes off. This time, I was not looking forward to it.

"I know what you're going to say." I said it as I walked into the bedroom as she closed the door.

"Oh yeah? What's that then?"

"You're going to tell me that we should just let them live here."

"No I'm not. Stay longer yes, and not giving them a deadline."

"If we didn't put a deadline on it they'll be here forever."

"Hardly! Come on, Charley will stay until she finds her next fella to move in with."

"Victim you mean."

"That's not fair. But okay. So that could happen anytime from tomorrow."

"Tomorrow until twenty years-time. Anyway, that would be worse, we'd just have your mum here then, getting older and grumpier and harder to look after. We'd probably actually *need* Charley then."

Kelly seemed to think this over for a few moments.

"Anyway, I'm not necessarily saying let them stay. I'm thinking we help them out financially."

"With what exactly? This wedd... Sorry, our wedding is costing a small fortune, I'm not exactly working my arse off for money and you don't exactly get paid in gold bars."

"I know, but there is the other little matter."

"What?" I honestly didn't know what she was getting at in the beginning, now I did. And in fairness to her, it was the first time she had brought it up since finding out about it. "Ahh, the land?"

She didn't respond to it. It looked like she didn't want to bring it up but felt she had to.

"That's what you mean isn't it?" I pressed.

"Well, it seems silly just sitting on it. I mean, it's completely your business and your choice but just think how comfortable we would be with that money."

"I get it, I do. Not many people know about it, in fact, you're one of only four living people that do including my lawyer. And my lawyer is the only other one that thinks I shouldn't sell it."

"Why not?"

"It goes up in value every year, why sell now. I see his point."

"But what if there's a crash or what if the lawyer is wrong, I mean, can you trust him?"

"Of course I can, he was my uncle's solicitor and I've known him years, he's always been good to me. Plus, it wouldn't make sense for him to get me to keep it as he would make more money from me if I sell it. Quite a bit actually."

"Okay, okay. I see what you mean. I don't get it, but I do understand."

"I think, at the end of this year, we can be ready to sell it. I just don't think I'm ready yet. It'll take a lot of adjustment you know, having money like that. We could move but would we want to? Quit our jobs but would we want to? Put your mum in a home, *because we will*."

She let a little smile creep onto her face. "Okay then, but."

"But what?"

"But, can we let mum and Char stay here until then then?"

"A year?!"

"Yeah come on? It's not *that* bad is it?"

"Kelly, it's fucking terrible! I feel like a guest in my own home. Not weeing in the night in case I see your mum riding the toilet in the crust again, or catching your sister taking a midnight bath, I want my life back, our life back."

"And you will have it, but just give it a while hey? This year we will be so occupied with the wedding we won't even notice how quick the time flies, I promise."

Jesus Christ. She was doing it again. And I was crumbling again. I thought I would just muster up enough fight to say no when she carried on.

"If you want to keep me happy and keep these in your life," She took out her boobs, "this is what I want. So it's either sell the land and buy a little house for them to rent from us or let them stay another ten to twelve months."

"Or?" I hadn't taken my eyes off her memory glands, even watching the little movement in them when she was making the points. Okay, I was a fickle man.

"Or, you don't see these again." And with that, she put them back in their cage.

It was blackmail, no getting away from it. But you should see these beauties! I'd folded again and they were allowed to stay. I made Kelly promise not to bring the sale of the land up until at least our honeymoon, which is where I said we could actually start making plans with it. She agreed and we went down to tell Cagney and Lacey the *good* news. Charley was so excited she said tomorrow night she was making curry for us all. Great, these two for months more and now my Friday night was going to spent gulping down a dodgy ruby. I'd have to make sure I had plenty to drink in.

I got in from work actually quite early on the Friday, I couldn't drag out any more jobs at work and my last job around 4pm actually dropped in the road next to mine, it wasn't worth taking another as I'd guarantee it would take me into the city or Cornwall or something, so I hit it on the head and went home. Normally that's perfect on a Friday, but my desire to make it home these days was about as desirable as sitting on a bicycle with no seat, it was gone. But I thought tonight, if I get home and start drinking, by the time this curry is ready I'll be well on my way to Merryville, I could eat and then pass-out.

Of course, this meant speaking to Iris and Charley. I could just go and sit in the garden; it was chilly but nice and bright. Mind you that would soon be going it was still getting dark pretty early. So my hope was that Iris would be sat at the table talking to Charley in the kitchen so I could sit in the front room and watch a bit of sport, or, if they were in the front room I could just sit in my dining room or kitchen and drink, I would sacrifice a bit of sport for that, I'd put the radio on or maybe a podcast. I had been listening to the Peter Crouch podcast for a while and it was pretty funny.

As I walked through my door I noticed the front room was empty, Iris' chair which she had now brought over was as sunken cushioned as ever, but, vacant. Bonus. I could nip upstairs, quick shower, comfy clothes and back down sat in front of Natalie Sawyer with a beer. I was about to leap up the first couple of stairs when my front room wall caught my eye. Where had my artwork gone? I say artwork, it was some nice bits of art that I liked and had framed so they all matched, and the room always looked fresh and modern. But not now. The walls were empty except for a couple of dodgy paintings with stained frames, not stained as in a nice varnish or faded colour, as in, things had definitely stuck to this over the years kind of stained. I'd noticed doilies with plants on them scattered around on the sideboard and shelves. Jesus Christ, what is that? There was a tartan throw over my sofa! Oh my god, there was a lamp stood in the corner by *the Iris chair,* it was hideous. It was quite tall with a faded dark green massive shade on it, with tassels hanging down of it. My god, I thought I was going to throw-up.

I ran upstairs as quickly as I could and planned to call Kelly. Then I decided not to. She could see for herself when she got here. I'd enjoy watching her face. Our fresh, modern but comfy, lovely living room was suddenly the set from *Heartbeat.*

I showered, almost laughing about it, I was in shock I suppose, but I wasn't going to say anything. I was thinking they were definitely doing things for a reaction for their own amusement. I headed back downstairs and it was still empty, I headed towards the kitchen, actually thinking maybe they had even gone out, bingo or something.

But I could start to hear a voice as I got closer and could already smell the curry, which actually gave me a pang of hunger so it must have smelt okay. Iris was sat at the table and was on the phone. I waved but got nothing back. I went into the kitchen to grab a beer and saw Charley.

"Alright chef?" Quality wit I thought.

"Prawns?"

"Prawns?"

"Yep, I got you some prawns. We don't like them so I'm doing you a different curry because Kelly said it was your favourite curry? That's right yeah?"

It wasn't but I appreciated the gesture, "Yeah sure, you didn't need to go to the trouble though."

"No trouble, I can make yours spicier too if you like?"

"Sure, not fire though yeah?! Beer?"

"Yeah why not."

I got two beers out and opened them and handed one to her. She had a big swig and continued stirring the saucepan;

"I'm doing rice, obviously but we'll have to order in the poppadums' and naan breads or whatever. I'm good but I'm not from Bombay."

"Nobody is anymore." I said, not really knowing why as I wanted to escape to the living room."

"What do you mean?"

"Nothing really. Just that well, there isn't a Bombay anymore."

"Yes there is. You can have Bombay potatoes."

"Well yeah, you can. Have you done them?" I did like them.

"No."

"Okay, never mind. I'll perhaps get some when we order the other stuff." I said and went to leave.

"See, you're not always right after all."

I should have just kept going but I couldn't quite do it.

"About what?" I said it politely and even added a little giggle-quaff at the end.

"Bombay. It's in India."

"I know, well, sort of I suppose but it's not called that anymore."

"Coarse' it bloody is."

"No, it's now called Mumbai. Has been since the nineties."

Charley looked perplexed. I told myself I liked telling people the useless stuff I knew to help them in the future regarding such conversations. In this instance, I just liked to see Charley stumped.

"I don't think that's right."

"Well, I'm sorry, but it is. Google it."

"Why change it?"

"Haven't a clue really. Something to do with the British colonialism legacy I'd guess."

"Why do you know so much about India? I know you like a curry but fuck me. You're a freak."

"Thanks."

"So, Mumbai is *now* the capital of India?"

"No, but neither was Bombay. So neither is Mumbai."

"What?"

"Delhi, or New Delhi I suppose, is."

"Mental. So it's always been Delhi?"

"Pretty much. I think it was Calcutta until the early nineteen hundreds but I'm not sure."

"Well I never. I feel extra pressure on my curry now I know *Ghandi's grandson* is eating it."

"Brilliant. Anyway, I'm going to head into the living room, unless you need me to do anything?"

"Nope all good here. Just letting it cook now, the hard work is done. Actually, crack me another beer would you?"

I did and got myself another to take through with me. Charley took the beer and smiled at me before saying;

"So, do you like your new front room?"

Now, was she doing this to get a reaction? Did she actually think the room had been improved? Surely it was a wind up.

"Yeah, no problem. I never particularly liked *Last of the Summer Wine* but at least now I know what it was like to be in it."

She didn't really respond, she just took another big swig of her beer, so I carried on;

"And you know it's not as if I have an impression to make bringing women back here or anything. Imagine bringing someone back here to that. They'd run a mile," I leant forward and patted her on the shoulder, "at least *I* don't have to worry about that."

She didn't like that much and couldn't help but show it.

"Yeah well, mum comes first, so that's all that matters. She wants to speak to you by the way."

Oh god.

"Oh yeah? About what?"

"Dunno."

"Who is she on the phone to?"

"Dunno."

The conversation had run its course it would have seemed and I made my way out of the kitchen, past Iris towards the living room of 1953. As I passed I had no idea who she was talking to but I was getting this end of the conversation.

"No, I'll be here a while now…. She's fine. She says she's happy but she's always been a bit of a closed book has our Kelly.

I slowed and looked at Iris. She continued talking and looking back at me;

"No, he's a taxi driver…. No, No she's given up on that dream…. Not really no…. Yeah, real shame…. Turning in his grave no doubt."

I'd heard enough and went into the front room, put the tele on and sat down with a sigh. I heard Iris say her goodbyes down the phone and I started to find the channel I wanted. I'd just found it after being sat down for about twenty seconds when I heard the voice.

"I want a word with you young man. Come in here."

I exhaled as loud as I possibly could and made it be known about my effort to get up from my comfortable position I'd instantly found sitting down. I got up, leaving my beer next to the sofa; I should have taken it with me;

"What can I do for you Iris?"

She pointed to the chair, "It's more about what I can do for you. Sit down."

I did as she requested and noticed Charley hovering around between the kitchen and the dining table. She gave me a smile that was the type of smile I'd expect a shark to give to a seal just before devouring it for breakfast,

"Now," she continued as I sat down, "I'm glad I've got you alone before Kelly gets back. I think it's probably the first time, no?"

It 100% was the first time, as I'd actually made damn sure it hadn't happened before now was all I was thinking, followed closely by the fact I should have stayed at work and then thirdly, quickly following, the fact I'd left my beer in the other room.

"I think so Iris. I can't just finish work when I like you see. I can't just throw a customer out because it's five o'clock."

"Five? I thought you worked til' six?!" Charley was sticking her nose in.

"Sometimes. How's that curry? Can I smell burning?"

"No. It's not on at the moment."

"Anyway," Iris was back getting my attention with a loud tap on the table, "before Kelly gets back I want to talk to you about your family."

I didn't know where this was coming from. "I don't really know that much about them Iris, except my uncl…."

"Not *that* family," she interrupted, "I couldn't care less if you were born in a palace or a cave, I'm talking about your family that you plan to have with my Kelly."

I was caught a bit on the hop here. "Erm, I don't really know. We haven't really talked *that* much about it. We plan to but when? We haven't got that far."

"Rubbish. You're getting married within a year of meeting her. You must intend to do everything quickly?"

"She did say he does *everything* too quickly if you know what I mean." It was Charley trying to be funny again.

"Can you stay in the kitchen sorting my curry please? Don't make me regret letting you cook tonight. It was touch and go you know."

"Hmm, touch and go? That's exactly what she calls you." Charley burned me again and finally disappeared into the kitchen. Now I just had to figure out what the hell this old bag in front of me was getting at.

"I'll get to the point," Iris said leaning forward, "I want a grandbaby."

My god where was this coming from? She didn't like me. And more importantly, why the hell did I leave my beer in there!? I delayed an answer, before struggling to an "erm, okay."

"No, not 'erm okay'. I'm old; I'm not getting any younger or any better. I'm a ticking bomb."

Not shit. Go and explode somewhere then.

"Right," I slowly said, still trying to understand what was going on, "and you want me to have a baby with her now? For *you*?"

"Yes."

At least she didn't beat around the bush.

"I think, Iris," I was still speaking slowly to try and figure out what to say, "I think, this year, maybe we will just focus on getting the wedding done shall we? Then *maybe* we'll start having a look at our options and plans over, I don't know, the next three to five years?" Why I was explaining this to her I had no idea.

"Well, let's just hope I last that long." I didn't answer. But she continued anyway; "It doesn't really matter because I will speak to Kelly this weekend. We know she makes the decisions anyway."

"Orrr... We just let us, as in, Kelly and I discuss it? In private. Like a normal couple would."

"Not good enough."

"Excuse me?"

"It's not good enough! I'll speak to Kelly about it. So with that in mind I wanted to speak to you about the conception."

Jesus Christ. This wasn't happening was it? Fuck my beer, I needed a scotch. And I'd never had a scotch before in my life. Mind you, I've never been sat down by someone older than a tortoise and been talked to about sex with their daughter. I had to figure out an escape.

"I think I'm okay Iris, thanks. I'm just going to g..."

"Sit back down! I'm not finished with you and it is rude to leave when somebody is talking to you. I just want to tell you the best positions to be in when you try and get pregnant. In case I'm not around, if you get your way, when it all starts."

"Iris, I'm not sure *I* want to be around when it all starts!"

She just ignored me and continued, "now, I can only assume you are enjoying sexual relations already? Before marriage." I just put my hand to my forehead and shook my head to myself. "Don't worry, I'm in a modern world and I understand so I won't judge."

"Thanks." Why the fuck am I thanking her?! Her other daughter gets bent over by barmen she's just met yet I'm living in sin.

"So, I've got this book for you." She reached down and pulled out a book. A well-worn book too. It was put on the table and I saw what book it was. I threw up a little in my mouth.

"The Karma Sutra Iris? Really?" I just looked at the cover without picking it up, "why is it so well used?"

She looked at me without an ounce of emotion and simply said, "me and my Jimmy used to have weekly interludes."

"Weekly hey? Good old Jimmy."

"When you're trying to conceive you need to get the right position so everything stays in there."

"Iris, please stop."

My plea was completely ignored. "And certain positions open up a woman's cervix better. It's a tough journey for the sperm on the way to the tubes so all the help that can be given, should be. And getting there involves getting through the possibly problematic cervix and its cervical mucus."

I managed to close my eyes and mouth but my god do I wish we could close our ears. She wasn't stopping.

"And fertility also is more likely should the woman orgasm."

"Is that actually true?" Charley was back again, I was wishing she would save me but she was revelling in it.

"It is true. A woman's vagina gets bigger and deeper the more she is excited."

"Oh. Like a wide-on?" Charley was surely taking the piss.

"I don't know what that is love but it sounds about right. So that's where this book comes in handy." She patted the book. This 70 year old woman, who was using words like sperm and cervical mucus, responding to wide-on questions was straight as you like. No smirks or chances of this being a wind-up. "Now, you can see I've dog-eared a few of the pages…"

"A lot of the pages." I interrupted as I picked up the book.

"Quite a few yes."

"Hang on, but you and Jimmy never…" I stopped myself. Did they know that I knew that she wasn't their biological mum?

"Never what?"

"Erm, never.. Never thought this book would bring so much knowledge and joy to others did you?"

"You're a weird man." Said Charley and was now sat down watching me squirm.

"I'm not convinced I'm currently the weirdest person in this room."

I was flicking through the pages without taking anything in. On purpose I was pretty sure.

"Now," Iris was leaning forward and pointing at the book, "the dog-eared pages are the ones you *don't* need."

"Right. Why is that?"

"Well, we won't go into that but they are more for fun, the pages not marked are the ones for optimal semen intrusion."

"So why are the other pages…." I stopped myself; I really just didn't want to know. "Thanks Iris, very thoughtful. I'll be sure to talk it through with Kelly later."

Iris looked pleased with herself. Did she really think this was normal? I couldn't lift me head up to look her in the eye or anything. I was broken man! Charley then grabbed the book out of my hand.

"Let's have a look then." She said as she took it out of my feeble quivering hands. Thankfully Iris got up and told us she was going to the toilet. She left mumbling something about how she had the runs and it wouldn't hurt to piss out her poo it was so runny. I didn't even get grossed out by it after what had just happened. Nor the fact we were having curry in a bit.

My attention went back to Charley who was flicking through each page saying things like 'yep, done that one, yep, ooh yeah I remember that one, that's tricky but worth it.' Then she turned the page to face me and asked if *'I'd ever tried that one? As it really helped me feel the bash of the balls when done right.'*

I got up from the table and walked into the kitchen, I grabbed another beer out of the fridge, forgetting or maybe just not caring that I had one in the sitting room, and I looked at the big pan of curry on the switched off hob and wondered;

Is it possible to drown yourself in pot of Thai green curry?

TWENTY EIGHT

Thankfully I managed to avoid talking to either of them again until Kelly came home. The only thing I got was when I was sat on the chair in the sitting room with my beer and watching tele, was after about forty minutes Iris walking back through telling me my toilet had just taken *one hell of a beating*. I just added to my list of things to remember if I ever needed to be sick and sat in silence until Kelly walked through the door. I didn't get chance to fill her in on my conversation from hell but certainly would do later.

The dinner was actually pretty nice. The conversation was pretty much Kelly and Charley talking about their days and a few bits and pieces about the hen-do. I had my separate curry, which had gone unnoticed by Kelly until Charley made her know that she had made a different one especially for me. I wanted to say that all she did was lob some prawns in the same sauce as you lot but it was a nice gesture so I didn't bother. What hadn't gone unnoticed was the fact it was a Thai curry, so the India chat we had earlier wasn't even bloody relevant!

We were coming towards the end of dinner when something hit me, like a sledgehammer. Kelly and Charley were talking about her hen-do, as they had been off and on all evening, with Iris occasionally adding things like, 'well, you look after yourselves over there' and 'Dublin is a lovely place *you'll* love it'. And for some reason, until now I hadn't even thought about the fact that Iris, obviously I suppose, wouldn't be going. I say obviously, I'm sure many women in their early seventies would love a little rave-up in Ireland but not this one. She looked over eighty, acted over ninety and behaved over a hundred. My main concern now though was the fact it would be just me and her for four days. I needed to recruit somebody to come and stay here. I was not dealing with naked, sitting on the bog the wrong-way-round, toilet cleaner covered, rude, karma sutra loving pensioner. I was drawing the line. Either that or I was drawing a gun and putting it to my head.

Later that night as we went to bed I filled Kelly in on my earlier chat with the love guru and she was just laughing away and telling me not to pay any attention to it. Easy for her to say. I also told her that I was going to pay somebody to come in and look after her mum when they were in Dublin. She told me not to be so silly and man-up. But I wasn't budging on this and told her to tell her mum, I wasn't man enough to tell her myself. The compromise was that we'd get somebody Iris knew to come and keep her company in the day, and the evenings would be fine because Iris would go to bed at seven each night apparently. I went along with it but would probably attempt to have people round or to head out on those nights. It would only be three nights, but four days, so at least that was taken care of.

At around about 3am in the night I had to get up and dash to the toilet. I didn't have time to check to coast was clear because this was an emergency! Luckily, it was clear and I made it there just in time. God knows what it was but I felt awful. Iris earlier saying about having the shits, was it a bug? I didn't think so as not long after I started being sick, Iris, as far as I knew, hadn't been sick. I was in the toilet, leaning over the sink whilst sat on the loo with it falling out of both ends, until about 6am that morning. I couldn't risk leaving, I'd never felt quite this ill. I woke up, in the bathroom just before 7 curled up on the floor, to the banging on the door. Luckily it was Kelly;

"What are you doing in there honey? Are you okay?"

I managed to figure out where I was and why before stuttering to an answer. "No."

"What's the matter? Can you open the door?"

"Kelly, you do not want to come in here, believe me."

"You been ill then?"

"Ill?! I'm ruined."

"Let me in then, let me see you."

"Kelly, I'm a costume of a man. There's nothing left of me. It's not a pretty sight."

"Come on, open up. It can't be that bad. What has caused it do you think?"

I opened the door and pulled her through into the odour-filled bathroom, she put her finger and thumb to her nose and muttered something.

"What do I *think* it is or what do I *know* it is?" I was whispering, mainly because I didn't want the two Herbert's to hear but also because it's all I could muster.

"What do you mean?" Kelly asked in a squeak as she still had her nose pinched together.

"I mean... I *think* it could be a crazy bug or virus, but I'm the only one in this mess. So therefore I *know* its food poisoning!"

"Oh blimey." Still squeaking so I pulled her hand away from her nose, "dodgy prawn do you think?" Her hand went straight back to cover her nose *and* her mouth this time. I think she could taste the smell.

"No, well yes probably. But I think Charley planted it! She's poisoned me!" It was in a loud whisper.

"Oh don't be so bloody dramatic. Of course she didn't."

"I'm telling you, she did. I'm certain."

"Why would she? What is her reasoning?"

"Reasoning? Seriously? The woman doesn't do reason. She's done this because she doesn't like me."

"Not this again! Jesus, I thought you two had sorted all this out." She was still talking from behind her hand. It was a weird discussion at the best of times to have. This didn't help but I couldn't blame her, it was putrid in here.

"Me too! But I reckon she has just been playing possum, just waiting for me to think everything was okay then wallop, she strikes!"

"You are mad. Of course she hasn't, you give her too much credit."

"I'm telling you."

"You got any proof?"

"Proof? Proof? The fact this room smells like a fifteenth century sewer should be proof enough?!!"

"That just proves you're, you're, a *little* under the weather."

"A little under the weather? I'm smack bang underneath the fucking storm Kelly." A noise crept out of my bottom that sounded a bit like when you squeeze the last of the ketchup out of a squeezable bottle. I just looked at Kelly. My eyes widened. "You had best go." It was like *a save yourself* moment.

"You don't need to tell me twice!" She ran to the door like she was trapped in a room with rabid bear.

I sat on the loo and let the only remaining bits of me exit whilst plotting my next move. I was convinced this was Charley. I just had to prove it.

I was out for the count for two days following this, this attack. I didn't think it was too harsh to say that. I couldn't get out and about but I put Rocket on the case. He knew pretty much everyone in Bromley. Especially shop workers as he did a lot of deliveries to them. All I wanted was him to make a few enquiries, see if anybody had been buying up dodgy prawns!

It turned out that he couldn't find anything out. The fish mongers told him they wouldn't sell off or out of date stuff whatsoever. I knew it was a bit of an ask but I had to try. I was getting better by the Monday but didn't go into work. I also didn't want to stay indoors with Myra Hindley around so I arranged to meet Rocket and Ethan for lunch. I wanted to run it past them some more. I'd stayed in bed until about 11am, when the landing and bathroom was definitely clear I went and showered, got dressed and started to leave the bedroom. I was really light-headed and had to sit down and take deep breaths. What had happened to my nice life?!

I got up and headed downstairs. I hadn't eaten for two days and I was starving. It was the first time I'd felt hunger and was glad to be meeting the boys at the Partridge pub, they did great pies. None of this dry toast, I was going straight in with the fattest pie I could find. My stomach was grumbling and my mouth watering at the thought as I headed straight to the door.

"Where you off to?" It was Iris. Sat happily in my formerly lovely sitting room, in her chair, blanket on her and the room already starting to smell of that stale biscuits smell.

"Just popping out to get something to eat Iris, haven't eaten for a couple of days you see."

"Thought I hadn't seen you for a little while. What happened to you?"

Your fucking crazy-arsed daughter happened to me I wanted to say but I saw Charley walking into the room from the dining room drying a plate.

"He's had a dodgy belly mum."

Iris laughed. "I thought so. The bathroom smells like a farm."

"Poor old Harry," Charley said, definitely mocking me, "what do you think caused it then."

"Not sure actually Charley. *Maybe* it was something I ate?"

"You don't eat that healthily do you?" Iris said whilst ramming a chocolate digestive in her mouth. Was that whole?!

"Think it was a home-cooked one this time."

Charley feigned a hand to her chest and said, "you're surely not suggesting it was the curry on Friday are you? We are all fine."

"Funny that." My hand was on the door handle and I should have just opened it and gone, but I didn't. "Thing is, my curry was a little different to yours wasn't it?"

"Can't trust those prawns I suppose. Bit of bad luck that. Isn't that right mum?"

"It is love. That's why I don't eat them. And *probably* why you shouldn't rely on others to cook your meals for you." In popped another biscuit.

"You mean like you do every single meal Iris?"

Through an almost full mouth, biscuit sprayed everywhere as I think she told me she *wished* she could still cook. But it might have been something about me being a cock. I wasn't sure.

Charley was now stood next to her mum and started rubbing her back. "Take it easy mum, for all intensive purposes, I think he's just making a point because he's been ill and he's upset."

I turned back towards the door, "I'm going and it's *for all intents and purposes.* How many times?"

"Sorry m'lord," Charley said, always trying getting the last word in.

"You're welcome." And I was out the door and basically running to my car.

TWENTY NINE

I made it to the pub, the traffic wasn't great so Ethan and Rocket were already there and had ordered. They'd phoned and asked what I'd wanted which was great as I now didn't have to wait as long if I ordered when I got there. And maybe wouldn't have to pay!

I spotted them as soon as I walked in and headed over.

"Jesus mate, you look a bit washed away." Ethan said as I sat down.

"Yep, rough couple of days. I reckon I've lost half a stone."

"This pie I ordered you will help with that," Rocket said, "Its £12.48 you owe me."

"£12.48?" The pies are £9.99 at lunchtimes?" I queried reaching in my pocket to get some money. Wasn't getting away with a freebie then.

"Yeah and I got you a coke as well."

"Thanks mate." I said and put £15 down. He took it but didn't give me any change.

"Maybe you should try getting poisoned Rocket, lose a bit of that timber?" Ethan said.

"All bought and paid for." He said giving his belly a bit of a wobble.

Our food came out and it was good. Not *Pie's from the Skies* good but just what the doctor ordered. Rocket filled me in on being able to dig any dirt up on Charley or dodgy prawns; I knew it was a long shot. I was going to have to accept defeat on this one. Again.

I was sick, literally, recently, of Charley and Iris and even talking about them was putting me in a bad mood. Luckily Rocket had a few things to discuss.

"So, I'm buying Mandy a ring next weekend and I'm going to make it official."

"Congratulations mate." We both said back.

"Trouble is I assume I'll just put it on her right hand, but how do I check that this is correct? Or do I get a big one and put it over the stump?"

"No Rocket. Please don't do that. Just get one for her, erm, right-handed ring finger I guess you'd call it." Ethan said as I put in my last mouthful of pie.

I started speaking before I'd finished my mouthful, channelling my inner Iris I thought. Even now the old bag wasn't far from my thoughts. "She knows you're getting engaged anyway doesn't she? Why not just ask her exactly what she wants? Even take her to pick it?"

"No, no, no my unromantic-esq caveman friend, I'm going for a full-on surprise."

"Well that's good. What's the plan?"

"The plan is to get the best God-damn blow job of my life she's going to be so excited."

"Oh for goodness sake." Ethan put his knife and fork down on his plate, with the not finished sausage (and mash) on and slid it away. "And I'm done with that."

"What's the plan with the proposal Rocket? Please, we don't need to know anything else."

Rocket shifted in his seat and started to tell us his plan with the giddy excitement of a ten-year old on Christmas Eve. "Well, I've booked us in at the Shard." He nodded and opened his eyes wide as he looked for our returned excitement.

"Very nice."

"It's a bit more than nice, but anyway, I'm going to get the waiter to come over with the ring in a glass of champagne."

"Nice. She drinking champagne at the mo? Being pregnant and all that."

"Shit!"

"It won't hurt, Rocket. Some women have a glass of red wine a couple of times a week when pregnant. A bit of champagne won't hurt."

"Maybe I'll get just one and drink it and catch it in my mouth and do it that way?"

"No Rocket, that's just weird." I said.

"And you'd probably just swallow it." Ethan added.

"Just stick with the plan Rocket, order the champagne without asking her and when it's on the table tell her you're celebrating. When she asks what, that's when you pop the big question."

He seemed to think about it for a few minutes before agreeing it was a good move. "It's her birthday too."

"Well, you could say the champagne is for her birthday as an excuse to order it?"

"I think I like the first way."

"Are you just doing this so you don't have to buy her a birthday present?" Ethan questioned.

Rocket just looked back. "How dare you. How very dare you!" It was in jest, "I love this woman and she is carrying my son and heir." Hopefully not in jest.

"Sorry mate. Thou doth apologise." Ethan bowed his head.

"No, anyway, I've got her tickets for her *actual* birthday present."

"Nice. Tickets for what?"

"She said she's a big Wimbledon fan so I've sorted some tickets."

"That's right I remember her saying. She loves Rafa Nadal doesn't she?" I said.

"Shitting hell mate, you've really gone all out! These tickets, a ring, the Shard, Champagne. You haven't cut back have you?!" Ethan added.

"Nothing but the best, you know me."

Ethan continued, "I mean champagne at the Shard? Got to be looking at a hundred and fifty to two hundred quid, never mind the meal!"

Rocket visibly gulped. "What?"

"Rocket, it's expensive. But worth it, it's a special moment."

"Fuck that. I'll take her to *Nandos.*"

"Don't be tight Rocket, just dig deep and brave the cost. It'll be worth it." We both encouraged him.

He mulled it over for a while. "I do really want that special blowy."

"Rocket, for fucksake, do it for other reasons maybe?"

"I'll do it for other reasons as well, not instead."

"Whatever Rocket. Anyway, how did you get the Wimbledon tickets? Hard to get them and expensive."

"Not really."

"What do you mean? Not really? I've tried for a couple of years, Claire loves it, especially Federer."

"Where does he play then?" Rocket asked.

"What?"

"I'm not very knowledgeable about it. Premier league football is all I bother with. No lower."

Ethan looked at me as I looked back at him. Before I asked Rocket if he had the tickets on him, he did and handed them to me and I held them for me and Ethan to look at.

"Rocket? This *isn't* what Mandy will have meant." I said.

"What do you mean?"

"Wimbledon vs Rochdale?" I shook my head. Then we both started laughing.

"What?"

"Nothing mate. You crack on."

The boys left as they had to get back to work. I didn't leave with them as I didn't want to go home. I could have worked but still didn't feel great. The thought crossed my mind to just stay in the pub and get hammered but decided I didn't even have the energy for that. I headed to my car and decided I'd go grab a Starbucks or something and give Kelly a call on the way, maybe see if she could get away from half hour or so. There was a shop not far from her work so I was hoping she would. She didn't answer but I headed there anyway. As I was parking up she called back;

"Sooo sorry about that honey, I was an office call. How you feeling?"

"No problem, I know you're a busy lady! Yep, I'm not so bad, I've just eaten and popping for a coffee. I just wondered if you were about."

"I'm not sure, I'm pretty busy. Where are you then?"

"I've actually just pulled up at the Starbucks just down from you."

"Hmm.. Okay, I'll be back at the office soon but will head straight down to you."

"Nice one, I won't keep you for long! What do you want? I'll order it."

"It'll have to be a quick chat and I'm pretty exhausted so you'd best get me a double-expresso please."

"Double-*espresso*?" I didn't actually pull her up on it but emphasised the 's' not 'x'. "Sure, it'll be ready when you get here; I'm just heading in the door."

I ordered the drinks and got them and found a table and waited. It was getting on for fifteen minutes. I didn't mind waiting for her, not only did it mean I was out of the house but I got to watch her arrive, I'd always be checking for blokes giving her the second glance they often did, and I'd smile. It was petty but I just couldn't help it.

I spotted her walking towards the door and I still got that little bit of a stomach flip every time I saw her. She came in and gave me a kiss and sat down taking her coffee.

"Arrrh that's good thanks babe, what a morning." She said with a big puff of an exhale.

"Busy then?"

"None stop."

"I thought that as you were a bit slow getting away. I thought you were in the office when I phoned as you said you were on the office phone. You needn't have bothered coming here if you were out with a client."

"Sorry, no, I wasn't in the office but I was only five minutes away. I think I must have meant I was on the phone to the office I guess. I can't remember, it's been a crazy morning!"

"Oh well, Monday is nearly out of the way. Listen, just a quick one, don't worry, I'm not going to moan about Statler and Waldorf back at home, but I wanted to say I'm going to meet with James, my solicitor this week."

"About the land?"

"Well, I'll have a chat about that but I'm going to speak to him about wills. Ethan brought it up last week in a text about how he and Claire have sorted theirs. It's morbid I know but I thought that maybe we should get ours done."

"Blimey. This is a bit doom and gloom isn't it? Do you think it's necessary?"

"Well, hopefully not but you never know."

"Bit heavy for a Monday this you know honey. But you're right, it's a good idea. Shall we talk later about it?"

"Yeah sure. I can't get hold of him at the moment anyway but maybe I'll book an appointment with him next week."

Kelly looked a bit, lost in thought, I guess you'd say. "What's up," I asked.

"Nothing."

"No come on, something is on your mind. It's not because I brought up dying is it?"

She put her hand on mine across the table, no don't be silly. I know it's a miserable thing to discuss but you're right. It's sensible."

"What's up then?"

"Well, it's just this solicitor of yours. I know you've known him a long time but you put an awful lot of trust and faith in him. I just think it's maybe wise to branch out a little?"

"How so? Do you mean about the land?"

"No , no. You're right, it's best he keeps in control of that, he seems to know what's best and you trust him with it. But you can get actual will-writing specialists for this and that makes more sense to me. It's just that, well, maybe it's because of the books I've read or films I've watched but if he's in charge of everything you own and then you get him to do the will, I don't know, it just doesn't seem right. He could easily screw you over."

I laughed but saw that she meant it. "Come on, seriously? There's an awful lot of laws and rules in place to stop things like that, even if you do know the solicitor or not."

"You're right. I'm just being paranoid. Silly even." She took her hand away and finished her drink. Then smiled at me.

"You know what, you're right. I'll find us a different solicitor and book us in next week, what do you think?"

She smiled and leant over and gave me a kiss, "I think I'm a lucky girl. You're the best."

"Well, you shouldn't thank me that much. I'm going to find a *fit* will-making lawyer to do it."

She stood up kissed my cheek and grabbed my balls in a tight squeeze, "you can find the fittest one in Britain if you like, but one ill-timed smile and I'm taking these."

"As if I could ever look at another woman!"

"That's my boy. Now get home and start getting my dinner ready, bitch." She winked and smiled and she left. I sat and finished my coffee smiling at the fact a woman like that even wanted to grab my balls.

THIRTY

Over the next few months there was plenty of ball grabbing but all in a good way. Kelly was in a great mood pretty much every day. I always went to bed next to her happy and woke up next to her happy. The bit in between the waking up and going to sleep with her I wasn't sure I liked so much. Saturdays and Sundays were always great as we would spend them together doing something. I'd meet Rocket and Ethan on Thursday evenings so Kelly could spend a bit of time with Charley and Iris ironing out her hen-do and wedding details. I avoided being home as much as possible in the week. I'd eat with them and take my abuse, even when I cooked, which was most nights. *Chicken is a bit tough* or *was this sauce made from that juice you end up with in the food bin* or a personal favourite, *these eggs look like you laid them.* I didn't know what more I could have done to keep these two miserable bastards happy but I'd long since given up on being polite. I was just rude back to them and didn't exchange any pleasantries. The only thing that got me through these weeks and months was Kelly. She kept me happy and kept me sane. I didn't even mind going to work these days. My customers perhaps weren't all that happy as all I did was moan about the gruesome twosome back home. I moaned so much one day that over the radio from the controller, the one that goes out to all cabs, told me that the last customer phoned to complain about me and that I should just kill my mother-in-law already! I think I'd pushed everyone to that stage with my moaning. I tried to change but every day she did something to piss me off. If I managed to avoid her for a day you could bet your life I'd bump into Charley and I'd just be as equally twatted off.

Kelly and I had sorted our wills after our coffee shop meet, I didn't find an attractive female one but Ed was a bloke that Kelly found and he sorted us out. We were leaving everything to each other, or future children. Ed made us put in a non-natural or accidental death clause or words to that effect, which basically meant if one of us were killed, committed suicide or died in suspicious circumstances the money wouldn't be released. It was a smart move he told us and we both agreed, apparently it was fairly common in wills involving potentially millions of pounds.

The only debate we had with each other was where the money would go should we both come a cropper. I was adamant that nothing go to Charley, or Iris for that matter, but I think we hoped we'd out-live her, and in the event of no living dependant we came to a compromise that it would go to a trust for any children of Rocket and Ethan. But ten percent of it would go to Charley. It was hard to argue but she started at twenty-five percent so I took it as a victory. On the understanding Charley would never know. That would be dangerous!

So the months started flying by and we were edging into July. The weather was good, which helped me because I spent a lot of time in the garden. I knew Iris wouldn't go out there so I set up a little bar in my shed with some seating and wired up a T.V. It was my little oasis. Kelly spent most of her time in there with me. And when she didn't, I'd just sit in there and chill out. I was asked a few times from friends about heating the place ready for winter. I would reply that we would have our house back by then because when we are back from our honeymoon they'd be gone!

We'd decided that once we'd cashed in on the land, we would actually stay here, sort out the old people's home décor, which now consumed the entire downstairs, we had a teapot, not just a teapot, and it had a cosy too. The dining room smelt like piss and biscuits, probably because all my lovely real-wood flooring had been covered by a shade of brown carpet, which I'm pretty sure Iris will have pee'd on several times, whether by accident or on purpose, who knew? The upstairs was just about okay, I'd never looked in Iris' room and the bathroom had handles attached in certain places and a tray that fitted across the bath but that was it. But we'd get it back to how we wanted it quick enough, which is why I let most of it go, as Kelly said, it was one year out of our next sixty together. Then we'd buy a little ground floor flat somewhere for Iris, and Charley if she was still about I suppose, there'd been no sign of a serious boyfriend so far. Then once Iris popped her clogs, we'd rent it out to somebody else's Granny and so on and so on. The rest of the money we hadn't talked about. I think Kelly planned to quit work and have a baby or two. Why not I thought, as long as she didn't spend her days doing baby-buggy yoga in the park and drinking coffee at forty two different coffee shops every day. Also we couldn't call our kids Tarquin and Libby or anything similar. I wanted Stan's and Sam's.

July was halfway through and Kelly was getting ready for Dublin. Her hen do. I was saying goodbye to her in the morning, their flight was early afternoon but you always wanted to get to the airport early and start with the fun. I was legitimately wishing her to have the best time. I was in a bit of an emotional state actually, not crying but this was the first time we'd have spent a night apart pretty much since we got together, and she was going for two! I didn't show her that I was sad to see her go, well, I did a little otherwise she'd think I didn't care, but from a selfish point of view, I didn't want her to go. Especially as Charley was in charge! Now Charley could do whatever or in fact whoever she liked as long as she didn't get Kelly in trouble. I trusted Kelly but I really didn't trust Charley. I wouldn't even put it past her to stage something and send me the photo. Luckily, Claire was going too and was taking Ethan's sister along as well. There were only six going in total so how much trouble could they possibly get into? Mandy probably would have gone too but being just about ready to drop ruled her out. She was actually due on the same date as my stag do but Rocket said he was coming no matter what. We'd see about that I thought.

The minibus that was taking them to Gatwick pulled up and I saw Claire and Natalie, who was Ethan's sister and two other girls I'd only briefly met, both worked with Kelly. I did wonder if she had many other friends but she simply said none that she'd like to share this with. There weren't even a lot of names on our wedding list that I didn't know, she always said that she never really had close friends, it was always pretty much just her and Charley. Other girls she hung around with, was a bit like the situation now, boyfriends' friends girlfriends. So why would you keep in touch with your exes friends girlfriends? I guess it made sense once you got your head around it.

I gave her a final kiss and a long hug and told her I loved her and to take it easy, *don't go mad* I think I said to which she replied *like you're not going to in Blackpool?!* She was right, I would go mad in Blackpool but that would probably be just to fit in. She got on the bus as Charley came out of the house.

"Laters' loser," she said as she passed me.

"Hang on." I requested and she stopped and turned back.

"What?"

"You know very well what. You be on your best behaviour and no stitch ups. Otherwise you're not coming back here."

"Whatever Grandad."

"I mean it. Obviously have a good time and get drunk but no stupid pranks. I know what women get up to on hen do's."

"Oh right, been on many have you?"

"No, but I've seen them and crossed paths with them plenty of times, they are a lot naughtier than stag do's!"

"I guess you'll never know about this one though. Shame that. Sleep well." She went to head to the bus.

"Remember I've got your mother here! She's my hostage." I shouted so the whole bus heard and gave me funny looks. I quickly added another sentence so I didn't sound too psychopathic, "and no licking whipped cream off men's cocks!" It didn't work, they looked even more disgusted as the bus pulled away.

I stood there waving them off thinking what an absolute fucking prick I just looked. When they were out of sight I turned around and there was Iris looking at me. I walked passed as she said to me; "You absolute moron." She may have been right. What a *fun* couple of days this was going to be.

It was Friday morning when they left and I straight away headed into work. The girl that was coming to sit with Iris for the day was already here. I don't know who she was or where Charley found her but as long as she kept Iris in tea and biscuits, getting her to the loo on time and didn't steal anything I didn't care.

Work went quickly, which these days, wasn't particularly a good thing. I'd heard from Kelly around 3pm to tell me they were in Dublin and she was already feeling a bit pissed. Apparently Charley was making them all drink *baby Guinness's* which I had no idea what they were but didn't think they were half pints of Guinness. But I told her to have a good evening and I'd speak to her in the morning. I was told to expect some drunken lovey-dovey texts later. Maybe even dirty ones. I don't know if that made me happy or not. She would be sat somewhere half-cut sending me sex texts and I'd be receiving them whilst sat opposite Iris, the hard-on killer.

It was around 8pm and we'd had dinner. I didn't sit with Iris, she sat with it on her lap and I sat at the table. She didn't thank me for any of it, not the making of it, the taking it to her and then taking the extremely empty plate away again. As the extremely empty plate was taken as she said to me; *bland.* But I didn't bite.

"So, how do you think they're getting on then?" I asked, trying to break the awkwardness.

"Pissed as farts, probably surrounded by randy men."

I should have expected that. "Yeah well, you know what Charley is like. Loves the attention."

"Aye. So does Kelly."

"Good job she's taken then." I said hoping that was that.

She dunked her hobnob in the tea I'd made her, again, without a thank you. Rocket said I should dip my knob in it first next time. Bit weird I thought, not to mention painful. He remembered that the time he did it that it was in water, not boiling hot tea. But he also added that he got caught, not in the act but the receiver (whomever it was) spotted things floating in it. It was one of my lesser favourite stories of his and there'd been a lot.

"Yeah," she started through a full mouthful again. If you sat in front of her it would be like putting your head in front of a gritting lorry. "Charley is sensible, she'll look after her."

There's more chance of Oscar Pistorious getting athletes foot was what I was thinking but I just nodded and excused myself to go upstairs to the bathroom. I didn't need to go but thought I'd stay up here until she took herself off to bed. Normally around 8:30-9pm.

I had a bit of time to kill so thought I may as well have a nosey in Charley's room. Is it out of order? I mean, it's my house and she is a grade-A wanker so I thought I was within my rights. Perfect opportunity too, she was in Ireland and Iris was deaf as a door post.

I don't know why but I slowly opened the door and was absolutely shitting myself. I realised I'd be a terrible burglar. My heart rate was through the roof, get a grip man! I wasn't sure what to expect as the door opened. That Thor's lookalike rotting corpse still tied to the bed, a pagan's worship station with shrunken heads smoking in the corner, a sex swing maybe? Turned out there was none of the above. In fact the room really was spotless. I headed in, flipped on the light and closed the door. I was going to be *that* nosey.

I'm not really sure what I was looking for, evidence that she has plans to do me in maybe, or perhaps I could unearth something to give me a bit of leverage against her. It was so bloody neat and tidy in here though I was scared to touch anything in case I didn't put it back right. And she'd go full Kathy Bates on me and snap my ankles like in Misery. I should have brought my phone in with me. I could have taken photos and known exactly where things went. Shit me, what was I even doing? I was losing the plot. I went to leave when I thought I'd just have a really quick look in her draws, maybe find a diary. I opened the top draw and it was full of bloody knickers and a sodding massive vibrator. Fair play. It should have put me off delving deeper but it didn't, I opened the next draw and saw nothing unusual, a few tops and skirts. There was a black wig in there too which was a bit odd but it was probably from a fancy dress party as there were a few more dressy-up things in the next couple of draws too. I let out a sigh and thought I was wasting my time.

I started heading towards the door, turning around just to check everything was how I left it and I saw something sticking out from under her pillow, I don't know how I missed it at first but headed over to it. It was a book so I opened it and saw it was all to do with our wedding. Plans from the start to the finish. Lots of detail and lots of effort and again I found myself thinking I was perhaps giving her too much of a harsh time. She was horrible to me but maybe she just wanted to protect her younger sister. Losing your parents at a young age would do that possibly. I felt like an absolute moron and put the book back and headed to the door, I switched off the light and opened the door. Straight into a completely naked Iris.

THIRTY ONE

It was terrible timing, quite literally the worst timing of anything since timing began. Luckily, she wasn't doing it in an attempt to seduce me, she was just walking to the bathroom from her bedroom, I guess for her delightful wash down, and I just happened to open the door, she had no idea I was in here.

"What the hell are you doing in there?" She turned to face me without an ounce of embarrassment. I wanted to tell her it was my house and I'd do whatever the fuck I wanted but I did also think I was actually in the wrong a little here.

"Erm," I had to think of something but all I could see was this naked pensioner, wondering how *so* much of her hung *so* low. "Kelly text and asked me to check that Charley hadn't left her hair straighteners on." It was feeble but I just wanted to get away.

"They are about ten hours into drinking and they suddenly remember this. I think the house might have already burned down don't you?"

"Probably Iris, who knows how the drunk-brain works hey. Sometimes you can't get something out of your head until you know for sure I suppose."

"Hmm, very strange."

"Well, in Home Alone his parents managed to leave him alone twice so you know, stranger things have happened." What the hell was I waffling about?

"I'll give Charley a quick call maybe just to check."

"Listen to me you miserable old bag, how about you do something good and take yourself and these *spaniels ears,*" I pointed back and forth to her flapping breasts, "for a wash then get into bed and lay there thinking of ways you could thank me tomorrow for all the dinners I've cooked you, the cups of tea I've made you, the *thousands* of biscuits I buy you not to mention the *fucking* roof I've put over your head," she went to say something but I didn't let her, "all for free! Not a penny have I asked for. The towels alone you get through have put me out over a hundred quid."

She looked back at me. I wasn't sure if she was going to hit me, cry, apologise, scream but in the end she just walked off to the bathroom. I went downstairs, glad to have the sitting room to myself and stuck on a movie. It started to play and I got a beer then I began to wonder what the next morning would bring. Hopefully I'd shouted some appreciation into her old bones.

I didn't get an apology. In fact, I didn't get another word out of her for the entire Saturday, I didn't spend much time there to be fair and when I got back, with Ethan around 6pm ready to cook all three of us dinner I saw that she already had a pizza delivered. I suppose to impose her hatred onto me she wouldn't accept my food anymore?!

I'd had a call off Kelly in the morning, she was hanging but was in good spirits, she told me she missed me and she was sorry she didn't get around to sending dirty text's, I told her that I assumed she had just passed out, which she had. She promised me a dirty text with maybe a picture later. I don't know why women always think this is what men wanted when they were away. I mean, she is one hundred percent right but at least let us ask for it.

That call, that Saturday morning had come at around 10am, I was already with Ethan and we were having breakfast in the café, then we were playing golf, couple of beers before back to mine for food, some sport on the T.V and a few more beers. Rocket wasn't able to join us. He didn't give a reason so that meant he wasn't allowed.

We were just arriving at golf so not more than an hour after Kelly had called she called back. It wasn't quite so pleasant this time. She asked me why I had been so horrible to her mum and how upset she is. She even said she was flying back because Charley was planning to, maybe to kill me.

I managed to talk her down and I explained the situation. I left out the snooping around Charley's room and said I just snapped because she had been so unappreciative. Kelly bought it as she knew I was struggling with it. Charley took more convincing but I managed it. Somehow I even managed to put myself into the position of having to apologise to Iris, but I thought maybe I should anyway. I mean, she is about a hundred and I was rude. Although, not incorrect.

Charley said she wouldn't come back early but she would be in contact with her mum every hour until she was back. Like I was some sort of torturer. This woman was living pretty comfortably, for free. Hardly a victim here.

I did apologise when I got in after the golf and a couple of beers. I planned on cooking something nice for her as an apology and asking her to put it behind us. I saw she had the pizza and told her my plan and how I was sorry. She accepted it and also, amazingly said she was sorry too. I didn't think that she had told Charley that I had been in her room either which was a bonus as it would involve another shit storm. Ethan looked on during this before heading to the kitchen.

"You're a bigger man than me." He said as I walked in there and cracked us open a couple of beers.

"Yeah, Claire said." I replied and he laughed and I made us some food, we ate it in the living room chatting away to Iris who actually looked pleased to be talking, mainly to Ethan, not so much me.

Ethan slept on the couch, as I didn't seem to have any spare rooms anymore. I woke up quite late realising how much I actually must have drunk yesterday. My head was pounding and I didn't remember getting to bed. Oh well. I looked at my phone and had a couple of missed calls and seven messages from Kelly. My heart jumped but not in a good way. There were voicemails too, I listened to them and luckily they were just drunk mushy ones from her, thank God. I let my breath out that I must have been holding and scrolled my way through the absolutely filthy messages she had send me. I wasn't complaining. Especially at the picture one!

I got up and had a shower which helped sort my head out a little bit. The girls were flying back early this morning, an error on behalf of Charley I thought, two days of drinking then up at 6am to catch a plane? No thanks. But it did mean Kelly would be back here nice and early. Maybe we could pub lunch it and have a good old Sunday afternoon out. It would obviously depend how knackered she was.

I was downstairs and chatting to Ethan, making breakfast for him and Iris and checking with my cabbie mate, who was driving the bus that was getting them, if he was there, was it on time, has he got them? In fact I didn't leave the poor bloke alone. Iris was in a decent mood, again, mainly because Ethan was here, I wasn't getting that much interaction, not that I minded, plus she seemed fairly happy so I was pleased Friday night was put behind us.

It was around 11am that my mate text to say he'd done the first drop and was now bringing *'the rest'* here now. He meant Kelly, Charley and Claire I assumed. Natalie lived in Croydon as did the other two that went so I assumed she'd have jumped out with them.

I informed the other two and said they'd be about fifteen minutes. We had another cup of tea and waited for the bus to turn up. When it did we went out the front to great them, well, great them like a bunch of wankers really, we'd only not seem them for one actual day but hey, it was love!

Claire was first off and ran to Ethan who scooped her up into a spin, *Jesus, they're years in and still pleased to see each other.* Iris said to me over my shoulder, *that's real love that.* Okay Iris I was thinking as I saw Kelly get out next. She looked tender but her smile said otherwise. She ran up to me and we kissed, I was going to pick her up and swing her round and knock Iris out but didn't have the bottle. I checked she was good and then saw Charley closing the sliding door on the van and heading over. Kelly squeezed my hand and told me to be nice.

"Hi Charley. You're looking….. right through me." I said as she marched straight past me whilst staring at me to the bone.

"Mum! Are you okay?" She said grabbing old covid in a hug.

"Oh Charley, it's been awful! He's such a horrible man" Iris responded as Charley left her arm around her shoulder and leading her indoors. Indoors to my house. That they both lived in rent free.

I didn't get any real gossip about the hen do, apparently even Charley was well behaved. We went down the pub that afternoon with Claire and Ethan but they were flaking around 6pm so we got a take away and went home. Maybe her hen do was tame, maybe it wasn't, it didn't really bother me. I was more worried that we were only two weeks away from my stag do and Blackpool.

It was that time. We were getting picked up and heading up to Blackpool. A coach with twenty-three southern softies heading up to Blackpool on a piss-up. The coach looked like the one that blows up on *Only Fools and Horses,* I wasn't even sure we'd get there. In fact, I hoped we didn't.

We left on the Friday morning, I said goodbye to Kelly at home as we had to meet at the pub to get the coach. The couple of weeks at home had been pretty toxic, Charley basically wasn't talking to me unless it was to have a go. She'd filled my shampoo with some sort of dye, obviously it was her but she denied it, but I was going to Blackpool with a very strange coloured head. Worst thing was, it looked like it had been done on purpose, luckily, I could pass it off as a stag prank. But it needed sorting first thing Monday morning.

The journey we were told would take at least six hours with a stop or two, but we had plenty of beer and a toilet on board. We also had Rocket. In the two weeks since Kelly got back, Mandy had had their baby. A little boy, Michael. We told him that this makes him Michael Michaels but he liked it. He was embracing his new role as a daddy but told us he was ready for this break. The baby was born on Wednesday, two days ago.

On the way up though he was telling us about *the music* he'd been working on. When we say working on, he wasn't creating music, he was basically making albums on Spotify. He thought he'd be the next *NOW that's what I call music* man. Crazy we all thought but he'd just say all it would take is one footballer or celebrity to clock it and it would go huge.

He was always adding hashtags and pushing it on all social media, even when it didn't work he was certainly persistent. This latest one though he was telling us was *THE* one.

"So boys," All the coach had stopped to listen to what he was going to say, because he made us, "the music you were just listening to was my latest little masterpiece, and I saw you all enjoying it. If I can ask you to follow it on all social media, share, retweet, send and all that.

Remember I'm the Rocketman so tell your friends, especially if they know Frank Lampard hey!" He laughed, "anyway yeah, Rocketman Album Party, spread the word, let's get it trending please, #rocketmanalbumparty. Let's get the party started! Make. Me. Famous."

Everyone started to talk amongst themselves again when Ethan called Rocket over;

"Erm, mate, you sure about that hashtag?"

"Yeah bruv' this is the one to penetrate the market."

"Penetrate is about right." I added.

"What?"

"Rocket, look at it," Ethan pointed at the hashtag, "it's got *'anal bum party'* in it."

A few lads sat near us heard and started laughing.

"Oh shit." And Rocket took himself off to the back of the coach thinking about his next big idea.

The rest of the journey was as you'd expect I suppose. Everyone got a little drunk, but only drunk enough to sober up quickly to go out to get drunk again. We had left around 10am and after hitting a bit of traffic and stopping for the obligatory ridiculously over-priced *Burger King* at the services we arrived just before 5pm. It was a long journey. If I was been completely honest I'd have gone and got a nice meal and been in bed for around 8pm the way I was feeling.

We literally threw our bags in the B&B and Rocket got his cousin to randomly put bags in rooms and said we'll sort out who sleeps where later by whosever bag is where. I guess it kind of made sense to save any arguments. I really wanted to ask about maybe freshening up, having a shower and getting dressed for the evening. I did attempt it but got shut down for being a tart. A tart? I was, as were most, in shorts, t-shirt and flip flops, not ideal for a Friday night in Blackpool I thought. Turns out we were probably some of the best dressed people there!

We headed straight to a place called the Flagship, which was like a busy party-bar all day and night. You really did lose all concept of time in there. After we had been in there about an hour I would have sworn it was midnight. There weren't any windows. It wasn't even 7pm though. I got dragged off to the toilet around this time and made to change into a baby. I had a nappy, a bonnet and a big dummy. I kept my flip flops but my t-shirt and shorts were thrown away! Nothing would annoy me more than that tonight, not even Rocket. I loved that t-shirt. Rocket said he'd buy me another tomorrow. He did, but it had *I love JLS* on the front. Which summed up Blackpool really. Strangely out of date, filled with absolute idiot blokes and loud women, but for some reason it's brilliant.

I got off quite lightly really that night, apart from being dressed as a baby and being made to do a few shots. Turns out being dressed as a baby doesn't even get a second glance in Blackpool. There were plenty of 6ft babies around, mankinis, smurfs, bananas, hotdogs, fairies; every fancy-dress stitch up you could think of you would see. But all this as well as families there with their young kids everywhere on their summer holidays. I was checking the pier's in case Little and Large or Cannon and Ball were on. It wouldn't have surprised me. I suppose the funniest thing of the night was towards the end when I was pretty much done, I got put in a room in one of the pubs with three other fully grown babies, two of them passed out and the other crawling about. I looked at them and sat down and drifted off to sleep myself. It was like we had been put in a crèche as the four now-mingled stag parties watched on and laughed.

I don't know how I got back to the B&B that night, a pram probably, but I woke up at 8am the next morning and felt right as rain. I was in a room on my own, there was a case that wasn't mine but I couldn't tell you who it belonged to but the other bed hadn't been slept in. I had a quick shower, in the shower down the hall, still with no sign of life anywhere else. I got back to my room and got dressed and decided to head out for a coffee and a newspaper, I wouldn't get breakfast as we would all meet up for that. As I headed for the front door I stuck my head into the lounge-bar that the B&B had. It was like a scene from a movie, in there, scattered around the room were six of my mates, three girls that had very little on, cuddled up between them and then Rocket, sprawled out across the pool table with a kebab on his face. I left them alone and opened the front door to head out. As I walked down the steps there was another mate asleep, on the steps. Then to the right, there was a bench in front of the B&B and there was Dean, asleep along the bench with his head on Gary's lap. But Gary was awake and eating a battered bit of cod, but holding and eating it like you would a mars bar or an ice cream;

"Alright mate?" I asked him, squinting as the sun was bright already.

"Sound mate yeah."

"What you got there?"

"This? Oh right yeah, cod I think."

"It's about half eight, where did you get it?"

"It's from last night. I saw it in the room there, still wrapped up. Cold but just fancied it."

"Righto. How long has Dean been asleep like that?"

"Oh. Erm. Hours like."

"So how did you get the fish?"

"I went the loo and saw it on the way back out. I thought, that'll do."

"And then what, you came back out here and put Dean's head back on your lap?"

"Yeah. Bless him."

I started walking off to the shop, "you're a lovely guy Gaz. Fucking weird but lovely. Do you want anything from the shop? Orange juice, newspaper, tartar sauce?"

"No I'm good cheers." He said thrusting the fish in the air in an appreciative gesture.

I walked to the shop and called Kelly. She was surprised out how well I sounded. And I did feel pretty good considering. I did wonder if I would get one of those delayed hangovers but I was pretty certain we'd be drinking again by the time it threatened to kick in.

On my walk back after a quick glance of the back pages I started to wonder what was in stall for me today. It didn't really worry or bother me, I noticed on the coach yesterday that Dan had a cowboy hat with him but hadn't really thought much about it. I found out that everyone else had told him Saturday was cowboy themed. He had bought this real cowboy hat, not the kiss me quick ones you can get everywhere here and what everyone else said they were getting, but a proper old fashioned cowboy hat. Not only that but he'd bought chaps and borrowed some cowboy boots. I don't know why they were stitching him up and not me? But it was going to be pretty funny.

I got back to the B&B and people were starting to get up and about. Back to front Bill was up and making tea, he is called back to front Bill because one time he came out in a Nike t-shirt on inside out, not even back to front despite his name, and when we asked him about it he said when he looks in the mirror he'd rather see the tick sign the right way as he'd paid the money for it. It only happened one time, the mad bastard, but he never lived it down. But it summed up the idiots I seemed to hang around with. He made me a cup of tea though and we sat and waited for the others to surface properly.

Rocket came down after his shower, probably to wash the chalk off himself, he was wearing some beige and brown stripped pyjamas and a green dressing gown.

"You looking for Gromit?" Dean asked him as he wandered towards us.

He just stuck his middle finger up and told us that he's a respectable father now so needed to dress appropriately. Like sleeping on pool tables and dressing like a Sunday league footballer that thinks he plays for Man United when going out is what we were all thinking as that's what he did.

We agreed we'd all get ready and meet at the café down the road at 10:30 then plan to be in the pub for 12. We told Dan 12:15. We managed to get through breakfast with everyone keeping it down despite a few pale faces and very slow struggled bites. We got back and got ready and went to the pub. Gary had taken Dan off to find a cash point earlier and deliberately got lost so we could get ready in our normal clothes, quite how normal mine would be I wasn't sure. We were in the pub, unbelievably it had the saloon style swing doors once you were through the main ones, God knows why but we found it hilarious. Gary and Dan were back at the B&B getting ready now and Gary made his excuses and said he needed the loo but Dan should go ahead. I don't know what he looked like walking down to the pub on his own dressed like John Wayne, then again, it was Blackpool. Perfectly normal. We were sat in the pub waiting for him to walk in and when he did it was one of the funniest things I have ever seen. He had gone to town! The saloon doors swung and in he came and instantly saw that he had been stitched up. *'But it's his fucking stag do!'* he squealed in a high pitch tone pointing at me. After that I heard someone say that that was a good point and I was picked up, stripped and put in a cow outfit. Udders n'all. I suppose the cowboy now had a cow to wrangle.

The rest of the weekend was pretty standard and I think I got away with a lot of potential pranks. The most shocking thing of the weekend for me was when Ethan sat me down towards the end of Saturday night and asked if I was ready for two week's time?

"Ready for what?" I slurred back.

"You're wedding idiot!"

Shit, yeah. It hadn't even hit me until now that I was getting married. I was nervous at the thought but the fact I was marrying the woman of my dreams made the excitement surge through my body. And as I looked around at the absolute meat-market I was in at the moment, blokes trying to pull, women trying to pull, tattoos everywhere on men and women, men were dressed I'm pretty sure in women's tops so tight you can see the ripples in their steroid enhanced muscles, with plunging necklines and tight jeans that stop halfway down their calves before seeing their sockless slip-on shoes, I was sat here dressed as a cow and I still wouldn't swap clothes with them.

Yes, married to Kelly this time in a fortnight? Abso-fucking-lutely.

THIRTY TWO

The next two weeks really dragged. I think it was the old case of when you're looking forward to something so much time seems to stand still. That plus the fact I had two weeks pretty much solidly dealing with Charley and Iris. Iris was basically just cutting me down every chance she got. Charley I had to actually talk to and give answers to as she was coming towards the end of her role as the *'wedding planner.'* Kelly asked me what we should get her for all her hard work. She laughed at first when I suggested a one way ticket to Australia. I was being serious.

On the flip side, even though the day wasn't quite here so it may still end up being a massive fuck-up, but so far Charley had done a good job. I had no interest in getting involved in the planning. As long as Kelly got what she wanted that was fine by me. Keep the bar well stocked and the speech's short and I'd be happy. It was only when Charley showed me the seating plan that I started to think maybe I should have been involved more.

"But all my mates are on the tables at the back." I pointed at the plan.

"They're rowdy." Charley said like it was a matter of fact.

"Who even are these people?" I was pointing at tables one and two. The tables right in front of the top table.

"Well, she went to school with both of us. We know her from church and this one here, Beryl, has known mum for forty years, and she's bringing three friends."

"What? Beryl and her three friends? It's £60 per head."

"Oh stop being tight."

"It's obviously too late to un-invite them but move them!" It wasn't a request.

"No." Charley said stubbornly.

"No? You will move them or I will remove the whole table."

"But Beryl can't hear very well."

"I don't care if she hasn't got any ears. I don't want the cast of *Cocoon* staring at me from three yards away. I don't even know who the fuck they are. And what church? When do you go to church?"

Kelly walked back in behind her as Charley started answering. She knew she was behind her though.

"Listen, what about I swap tables one and two around, that way all of Kelly's fit friends will be sat right in front of you."

"What's this?" Kelly heard, obviously, and headed over.

"H wants a better view when eating his dinner next to his new wife."

"No I don't! And don't call me 'H'. I simply don't get why Beryl, Maud, Tiffany and Hilary are getting better seats than Dean and the boys."

"You've got Rocket and Ethan on the top table with you. What more do you want?" Charley responded

"Where's Mandy then?"

"I've put her here. You see my diagram? Just a fork."

"You're such a cow." Not my harshest ever put down.

"Ooooh. Watch out."

"Hang on, Rocket and Ethan are on the top table next to Kelly. And I've got Iris and you next to me?! No fucking way."

"It's tradition you miserable prick. Are you trying to ruin this poor girls big day." She put her arm around Kelly.

"It is tradition honey." Kelly said through her sorrowful eyes.

"Fine, do whatever the fuck you like." And I turned to storm off.

"Thanks honey, you're the best!" Kelly said after me before I heard Charley add;

"Told you I'd make sure it weren't a problem." I'd heard her and I turned back around.

"And just to let you know, if you and your scabby mum are going to be sat next to me and the *Golden Girls* sat opposite, do you know what I'm going to do? I'm going to *finger* her during pudding." I said pointing at Kelly.

"Hang on a minute!" Kelly protested and held her hands up, we both looked at her, "you could at least use my name."

Charley and Kelly both laughed out loud. I'd had enough, I stormed out again.

Was it too late to run away?

My mood had eased by the time we went to bed. It was two days before the wedding and the last night we'd spend together before getting married as I was staying at Ethan's tomorrow with Rocket. Claire and Mandy would stay here. So no way was I staying moody, I wanted some action! And got it.

The night before the wedding was a little bit different. We didn't spend it getting drunk and talking about former conquests or what could have happened, we spent it taking turns trying to get the baby to sleep. Rocket lost the argument about Mandy taking the baby because he was a boy baby. Therefore, included on the male side of tonight's proceedings. So, as he didn't like sleeping for more than about seven minutes at a time, the three of us took turns trying to rock him to sleep or singing little melodies. It probably looked like a real budget version of *Three Men and a Baby*.

But it did mean I got to bed with a fresh head and actually get a decent night's sleep, thanks to my ear plugs and the fact I told Rocket I was off the clock at midnight from babysitting.

141

I'm not sure how much he slept but he was up before me, probably because of the baby. He made us breakfast and we got ready. Mandy's mum picked the baby up, it was his first overnight stay away and Mandy wasn't going to drink just in case apparently. Rocket said he was taking beer to the church.

We were dressed in out suits and in the car and we were on our way. Next stop would be the church. Nerves hit me, but I didn't think it was because of saying my vows, doing my speech or even seeing Kelly. It was the fact I was about to become related to Aileen Wuornos and her mother.

I put all that sort of shit to the back of my mind and tried to concentrate on the fact I was about to marry the perfect woman. Officially removing her from the shelf I think a mate said on the stag do, whatever that means. *'Yeah and she is real top shelf material'* Rocket added. I don't know if he meant she was a real beauty so she was top shelf or if he meant she'd look good in a top shelf porn magazine. Probably the latter knowing him.

I was now stood at the front of the church as the organ started to play I had a real ripple of nerves flow through my body. Ethan was slightly behind me to the right and put a reassuring hand on my shoulder and then Rocket next to him, when he muttered the words *fuck me* I thought it was time I turned around too.

As I did I saw Kelly walking up the aisle looking simply breath-taking, I mean, I literally had to grab an extra breath. She was in an elegant, tight-fitting, strapless, understated dress that looked like it was made for her, in fact, it probably was, but however much it cost it was worth every penny. She was carrying a simple bouquet of white flowers and had the biggest smile on her face I'd ever seen. She was made for this moment. And I was reaping the rewards from it. She was alone coming up the aisle, I don't know why I hadn't actually thought about that, who would give her away or walk her down the aisle but I don't suppose it bothered me as long as she got to the end. And got to me.

I did notice Charley, in a very close to white bridesmaid dress which I thought was a bit weird, about ten yards behind her walking up slowly with Iris holding her arm. Iris had her hair cut short and styled, God knows how much lacquer she had to hold in place but she looked like Rod Stewart. Even walking next to and linking arms a 30 year-old, good-looking woman made this even more the case.

Kelly was now next to me, we said hi through our massive smiles and the service was underway. When asked who gives this woman away, Iris grunted something in the way of that's me and went to take her seat on the front pew. The vicar actually said thank you Sir to her, which made my day. Well, not made my day but certainly added towards loving the day. Kelly and I were now facing each other reciting our vows and we are back to where the story began. I should have been thinking I'm the luckiest man in the world but I just couldn't get either Charley or Iris and their matching snarls away from line of sight.

But we got through it, I got my first kiss as a taken man and we were off to the reception. That all went really well, lots of drink was consumed and people had a good time. Well most did.

"Who actually thinks veggie burgers are a good idea?" I heard Iris say to Kelly. I don't know why she ordered a fancy 'deconstructed vegetable burger' when she put her order in weeks ago but she did.

"Cows do mum." Charley responded, maybe taking it personally as she decided on that as the veggie option for people. Iris boiled bacon and spooned corned beef and spam into her mouth from the tin normally so why she ordered it really baffled me.

Kelly kept checking with me that I was okay and I kept checking on her too, we really were happy and enjoying the day. Then Charley asked if she could have a word in private with me;

"What is it?" I asked as we stepped just outside the room.

"Just so you know, with you two going on your honeymoon tomorrow that your house will be in safe hands for two weeks."

"Is that it?"

"And, I wanted to thank you for my present too."

"No problem." And I went to leave, "Hang on, what present?"

"For sorting the wedding."

"Yeah, but what did we get you? Kelly hasn't said."

"A week in Corfu."

"Really?"

"Yes, why? I go a week after you get back."

"So, it will actually be three out of four weeks without you? No problem, you are more than welcome."

"I can't believe Kelly didn't tell you. That's a bit weird, especially as you're married." She was trying, and failing to stir the pot.

"It is a bit weird. Shame though, if she'd have brought it up with me I'd have paid for two weeks." I smiled the falsest smile I could and walked off.

"You'll be charge of mum!" She yelled, "Kelly has a week's training course that week don't forget."

Shit, I had forgotten. She had a week in Manchester on a course, we moaned about it but then decided it would be good to get it out of the way as soon as she was back. But I didn't want to show Charley that I was annoyed.

"Yep, not a problem. Me and Iris are like this these days." I said crossing my fingers.

"More like this." Charley said giving me the V-sign.

"No, that's your legs. Who is the unlucky victim tonight going to be?"

"Drop dead! I'll make sure my mum is on her worst behaviour."

"What's new?!"

"If she doesn't make your life hell, I certainly will when I get back. Mark my words."

I walked up close to her, "What is your problem? I mean your *actual* problem with me? Is it because Kelly loves me and you're losing her and getting left with your crusty old mum? Or is it just because I'm a man?"

She got right up in my face, "All of it!"

I pulled away, maybe because I thought she might bite my nose off or head-butt me, "well I can't help that can I. But I do want you out of my house, you and that wrinkly sack of shit out there. Both. Out. In one month."

"Good luck with getting that past Kelly!"

"I don't give a shit. We are married, she's not going to run away, she's with me forever, don't know if you noticed that today? Til' death do us part." I saw her face and realised I shouldn't have said that.

"Well, I didn't realise there was a get out clause."

"Stop being so dramatic. Just start looking for a place. Kelly will provide the deposit from MY money. You're fucking welcome."

"I like where I am."

"Just drop it Charley. You're gone."

"Not without a fight. It's a doggy dog world out there. We'll see what happens."

"Alright Snoop, yeah we will see. Its *dog eat dog* you absolute weapon." And with that I left.

I was back in main room trying to take deep breaths and gain some composure. I stayed on my own and found a seat for a minute. I looked up and saw Kelly, she was just gliding around the room enjoying every moment. She was so good with people and people instantly just took to her. It wasn't a huge wedding and most guests were here because they knew me, and now Kelly in most cases, but apart from the table of old farts, a few people from her work and another couple of school friends the rest were my friends originally. I was almost one hundred percent certain that it was because of Iris and Charley that people didn't last in their lives. I reckon the only way Iris managed to keep Kelly in her life was because she was a hostage. Blimey, imagine being held hostage by Iris? What are your demands to release the prisoner? *A jar of Horlicks, a cucumber sandwich and a helicopter to Eastbourne!* It didn't bare thinking about.

I decided not to move for a while as I just watched Kelly. I couldn't help it, she was magnificent in every way, she was just one of those people, how on earth she was related to Charley, not only related but friends with I will never know. After about ten minutes I got up and headed over to grab my wife, we had done the speeches, Rocket's was actually decent and was complimentary of both me and Kelly as was Ethan's. There wasn't a father of the bride so Kelly got up at the same time as me and said a little bit before I gave my little bit. I sat back down as Kelly thanked Charley for her hard work, it was now getting near our first dance time, but first we cut the cake. We danced to *Wonderful Tonight* by Eric Clapton, it was awfully nerve-wracking but Kelly go me through it. *Then* after all the fun and the drunk blabbering's you get towards the end of a wedding I lead my new wife up to our bridal suite. And we had a night to remember. Even though I stopped short at calling her Mrs Cahill, that just sounded weird.

The next morning we woke up and both still had big smiles on our faces;

"Good morning husband." Kelly said and pulled me in for a kiss.

"Good morning the wife!"

The smile disappeared from her face, "oh my, you're right! I'm a wife. The missus' or the ol' ball 'n' chain huh?"

I pulled her in for another kiss, "if you're the ball and chain you can keep me as your prisoner for the next fifty years or so."

She smiled. "Deal! I can't believe yesterday is over though. What a day! Do you think everyone had fun?"

"I do, absolutely. So you can smile again. Yesterday may me over but what about this being the first day of the rest of our lives?"

"I know, I know and I can't wait. I just wish we could re-do yesterday again."

"Well, we'll have the DVD of it soon enough so you can watch it every day if you like?"

"Yeah you're right."

"So what do you want to do today?"

"Erm, well Mr Cahill, how about you fly me to the Maldives?!" With that she was on top of me and the smiles were well and truly back.

THIRTY THREE

We said our goodbyes and left for the airport. I warned Charley that she was on a countdown clock and it wasn't to be forgotten. We landed in the Maldives after a fairly decent ten or so hour flight, excitement I suppose, and we were well within our rights to be excited, what a place. We got a sea plane to our island which only had thirty-six dwellings on it, so we assumed seventy-two guests. Tiny. But it did have three lively bars and five perfect restaurants. The cocktails and lobster were destroyed over the two weeks. We also discussed the plan with the money. I had sanctioned the sale a while back and James managed to get a bidding war going so we were due in excess of ten million! Not bad I suppose. Everything had run smoothly and we hoped to have the money through not long after we were back from here. We had decided we would stay in our house, do a little revamp once the other two muppets had left, buy a new car for me and maybe look for a new career or investment in something and Kelly would try and get pregnant and, what was her favourite bit, quit work. I told Kelly that my life seems to have changed somewhat in the last year or so. I was a taxi driver in Bromley spending my weekends with my mates at the pub just coasting along, now here I am, sat on paradise beach happily in marital bliss with a truly beautiful wife, who rocked a bikini, talking about what to do with ten million quid. Like that George Best story, it really was a *'where did it all go wrong'* George moment.

It came crashing back down to earth literally as our wheels touched down back at Heathrow, as we switched our phones on (after two weeks of not having them, which was brilliant) and we got message after message from Charley telling us there was an emergency. All from today. Kelly phoned her and was told to calm herself down as it wasn't as much of an emergency as Charley made out and she'd tell us when we got home. I had a feeling I wasn't going to like it.

"Rats!" Charley said as we walked in the door.

"Nice to see you too sis." Kelly said giving her a hug. "What are you talking about?"

"We've got rats!"

"What? Where?" Kelly jumped up on the sofa

"Everywhere!"

I put our cases down and asked what she was going on about.

"We have got rats, they're all over the place, upstairs, downstairs, everywhere. I've seen three of them in the last hour."

"Okay, well, I'll call the exterminator."

"No."

"No? No what?"

"You can't use them, they spray stuff that will affect mum and her medicine."

"What are you talking about?"

"They use a spray to disorientate them then they get them and kill them."

"And?"

"It will mess mum up!"

"So? They are only here because that wrinkly bit of old cheese doesn't move."

"Charming. I'm going to get them myself though. I can order this poison online, it makes one of them eat it and take it back to its nest and it kills them all, I read about it."

"Fine, whatever. So did you order it?"

"No. I need a bank card."

"Honestly, you're like a twelve year old. Here you go, order it and give it me back. You have until I put these cases upstairs so get a move on." I handed her the card and asked Kelly to watch her as I took the cases upstairs. "No shopping!"

Over the next week or so I was counting down the days until Charley was off for a week sunning and shagging herself senseless. It did mean that I wouldn't see Kelly for a week too, or at least the Monday to Friday of it and Charley was going on the Sunday, so I'd see Kelly off on the Monday at the train station and meet her there on Friday so I was telling myself it was only actually three days of not seeing her. And as a bonus I hadn't seen a rat in this time around the house either. Whether Charley was winding me up or whether the poison that arrived the next day had worked I wasn't sure.

It was Sunday and I was glad to see Charley go, yes Iris would be here but at least I could get away from her, Charley seemed to be everywhere. Before she left she told me that her mum has a lactose problem, like I didn't know but there was some powdered milk in a tin that I'd have to use now in all of her seventy three cups of tea a day instead of real milk. Fine, just get lost will you was all I could think. She took ages to leave, she must have been in with her mum for a good twenty minutes even though she had a plane to catch. I knew she spent a lot of time with Iris but come on, you're gone for a week, I'll make sure the rats don't eat her. Maybe.

Finally she was in the passenger seat of Kelly's car and they were ready to go. Charley was actually crying. Such a weird woman.

"You can take her with you if you want? Hire her one of those Benidorm-style scooters, I hear Corfu is great for bingo and serving pilchards."

"Go fuck yourself."

I tried shouting after the car that her sister was too busy doing that for me but I don't think she heard. Sophie, my elderly neighbour did though as she was out in her garden. She just looked at me.

"Sophie…" I said with a wave and putting my head down, I walked back in the house.

"Right Iris," she was in floods of tears too! "Come on, she'll be back in a week. How about a nice cup of tea?"

The next morning was actually really hard. Saying goodbye to Kelly, or my wife I should say now was really tough. I had to get into work, as a regular had asked me for lift to the airport so Kelly had to get herself to the train station, which was a shame as I pictured a real movie moment when I could run down the platform after the train waving at her as she is leaning out of the window. Okay, it's not 1935 and we don't have steam trains here but that's what I pictured.

I did my airport run and checked my phone to see a picture from Kelly sat on the train with a miserable face telling me she loved me. It was strange having a feeling of sheer bliss inside you, sure this week was going to be hard but there was also no Charley, the money from the sale had come through and been placed in an account set up by my solicitor, whilst we decided what to do with it. Don't worry, she may be my wife and I love her but you still needed both of us to get anything out of that account. I wasn't that silly.

I spent the rest of the day at work. I got a call off Kelly saying she had arrived at her hotel and later did a video call to show me her hotel was pretty nice, but it was quite near *the Printworks* so she was just going to *have* to go out with some of the others who were on the course. I checked that there were no good looking men and told her to have fun. You can never relax having a pretty wife though. You can trust her all you like but you can't trust sleazy men, when they linger their hands on girls bums as they go past, or squeeze the gap so the woman has to get through and her boobs or bum have to touch them, I knew them all, after all I'd grown up watching Rocket.

Iris was quiet so I made her a cup of tea after dinner and she said she was going to bed. Honestly she needed to grow up, in her seventies and moping around like a teenager because her crazy daughter has gone away for a week.

She hadn't even cheered up the next day. I wasn't working today or the rest of the week, I said it was so I could look after Iris but really it was because I was looking for places to move them into whilst also thinking how to redesign the house. Obviously any ideas will now need Kelly's approval but that was exciting in itself.

"What about this place Iris? It's already got a stair lift."

From her doze she just mumbled the word 'whatever'. Was it my responsibility to cheer the miserable old crow up? How would I cheer her up? I made her a cup of tea and went back to my planning.

I made Iris dinner and she went straight to bed after it again. I didn't mind as it meant I could relax in the sitting room and watch something violent. Which I did. I spoke to Kelly who said she was off out for a meal tonight and the course was boring. I told her that her mum was moping about and asked if there was anything I should do but she told me that she is like this whenever Charley isn't around. We said our goodbyes and I told her to text me in the morning.

I didn't sleep all that well. I was definitely missing her, but at least tomorrow there would only be one more whole day. I wondered what Charley was getting up to and gave a shudder, some poor lad out there was getting it that was for sure. Good or bad it didn't matter.

The next morning I was up and about ready to finally sort a place for those two to rent whilst I looked to buy another which they could then rent from us. It wasn't ideal but it made sense. I just couldn't hang on for a sale to go through with them both still living here. I actually wasn't worried about Charley and her threats anymore, but I could see it affecting me and Kelly, and that was the last thing I wanted.

I'd made Iris her tea and put in next to her chair as always and waited for her to come down but she never did. She was through that living room door at 8.45 every morning like clockwork. It was 9.30 now and still no sign. Dozy old cow has probably washed herself with bleach or something so I shouted up the stairs;

"IRIS!? It's 9.30! Breakfast." No reply.

"IRIS!?" Still nothing, I shouted again as I walked up the stairs, again with no response. I knocked on her door and shouted again. Still nothing, had she gone out? She never went out. I slowly opened the door still saying her name;

"Iris? You in here?" I opened the door and stuck my head round and there she was. Still fast asleep. Hard life sat watching television, drinking tea and eating biscuits I thought as I headed over to give her a shake.

"Iris, time to wake up, those malted milks won't eat themselves." But, as I nudged her arm it flopped down the side of the bed. I noticed she was very pale. And now I realised, she wasn't breathing. She was dead.

After the initial shock and not knowing what to do, I tried shaking her and tried to find a pulse but she was long gone. Probably late last night was my completely T.V hospital drama watched diagnosis. I called the doctor and he said he would be there within twenty minutes. No need for an ambulance. Even though I didn't like her and she certainly didn't like me, I got back downstairs and burst into tears. I didn't know why I was so upset, I suppose I am just a human being but the thought of Kelly finding out this news made me more upset. And Charley finding out? Shit, I was actually a bit worried what she might do to me.

I phoned Kelly but it went straight to voicemail so I left a message, for her to call me back ASAP, not a message that her mum had died. When she did return my call all bubbly and happy, I had to tell her and listen to the happiness ebb away and the tears and screams starting. I just wanted to hold her. She said she was leaving now to get the first train home.

It was a long few hours as I waited for her to get back. The body had been taken after the death certificate had been issued so I sat and waited for Kelly to get back. When she did she ran in and just gave me a huge hug whilst letting out screams and tears. After she calmed down we got a vodka each and sat at the table and discussed what had happened. She was upset she wasn't here but realised there wasn't much that could be done, when your time is here it's here and Iris was not a well woman. Of course the main problem now was Charley. Kelly said she'd call and tell her. I wanted to be around for support but also as far away as possible when she told her and definitely far away when she got back here.

I listened in on the call and heard the screams from the other end and the tears of Kelly start again, then split ends of a staggered conversation of things from Kelly like ' no he didn't, don't be so stupid and no, you're not going to kill him'. I expected it really. She said she would get the first flight back she could.

That night Kelly and I pretty much sat in silence, she spent it sat in Iris' chair just stroking the arm. I was thinking about getting a skip. We went to bed again in relative silence with me just breaking it every so often asking if she was okay or if she needed anything. She said she was fine before finally falling asleep, probably from exhaustion but cuddling me for comfort.

Charley couldn't get a flight back until the Saturday so Kelly and I sorted various bits out. Iris was being kept at the hospital as the funeral home couldn't take the body until Monday as we were told there had been an autopsy. The coroner couldn't find a cause of death so wanted to find it out. I'd never really thought about old age death before. When people say that somebody died of old age that can't be an official reason can it? Surely something packs in and causes it? This was obviously what the coroner wanted to know. It wasn't nice for Kelly to hear or even picture as we all knew what it involved but it would be for the best.

We were actually in the hospital collecting Iris' belongings on the Saturday when Charley turned up. Good place to be I thought, there's witnesses and if she stabbed me, at least I was in a hospital!

She stormed in, her eyes raw with red and hit me as hard as she could whilst screaming *murderer* at me. She unloaded as much verbal and physical abuse as possible on me, which seemed to last for ages but was probably about thirty seconds until security came and grabbed her off me, I noticed Kelly screaming back at her to leave me alone. I had blood running down my face from my nose and my eye already felt like it was swelling. Charley was getting taken away by security still kicking out and screaming at me being a murderer. Kelly was telling her to come back when she had calmed down then checked that I was okay. God knows what she had in her hand when she hit me but it cut me open pretty good. I was taken into a cubicle and cleaned up and actually got given a few stitches. Kelly was in there holding my hand the whole time telling me not to worry about Charley, she will come around soon. I took the fact that Kelly had stayed with me, reassuring me and not chased after Charley as a victory. Okay maybe it wasn't the best time to be petty but there were going to be some big battles ahead. We sat around in the hospital for another hour or so, we heard from security that they had let Charley down to see the body and that they hadn't called the police but they would if it happened again.

Shortly after an hour we noticed Charley coming down the corridor towards us, she was definitely calmer but I didn't trust that, was it an act. She had just seen her dead mother for the first time so who knew what was going on in her disturbed mind.

She got near us but not that close as security lurked;

"You." She pointed at me, "you did this."

"Charley," Kelly said, "don't be so stupid, mum was just old. It was her time."

"Bullshit. He did it and he couldn't wait to do it, what did you do? Put a pillow over her face that night?!"

"Charley!" Kelly yelled as I just shook my head, amazed anybody, even Charley would think me capable of such a thing.

"Why are you defending him? Because I was mums favourite?! You're as bad as him."

"Charley, you need to go home and get some sleep, I bet you have been awake for seventy two hours or more?" Kelly tried to reason.

"Go back to Jeffery Dahmer's house here? Are you joking? He'll kill me next." Her voice was getting louder.

"Lower your voice, they will call the police."

"GOOD! Then they can arrest him!" she screamed again pointing at me. "Couldn't wait could you? Get me away on holiday so you could bump her off hey? Well, I'm on to you!"

"Charley, listen," I finally found my voice, "I know you're upset, so are we but you need to calm down."

"Don't you fucking dare tell me to calm down! I'm getting you for this, just you watch. Fucking sending me to Corfu so you could suffocate a poor defenceless old lady."

Lady was a push.

"It was my idea Charley to send you on holiday remember? Harry didn't even know about it."

She stopped and paused for a minute and then came closer. The security moved in closer too. "Well you're in it together. Bonnie and fucking Clive here!" Hmm, do I tell her? Best not. She carried on, "I'm going to get you. Both of you. Before the police do, I'm going to get you." It was probably the most sinister sentence I'd ever had said to me and it really did scare me.

She walked away just nodding her head up and down looking at both of us, then she did the thumb across the throat gesture, turned and walked out the main door.

I grabbed Kelly in a tight hug and checked she was okay. She was and said she had never seen her like that. I told her she would be okay once she calmed down and saw sense. It did worry me that Kelly didn't instantly agree with me.

"Come on, let's get home." I said, hoping that Charley wasn't heading back there. As if reading my mind Kelly asked if we could go to a hotel instead. Too bloody right we can I thought but said if it made her feel better and safer we would.

We walked out into the dark evening and drove to a hotel miles outside of Bromley.

THIRTY FOUR

We woke up next morning and tried to decide what to do. We actually booked the Sunday night too and decided not to risk heading back to the house yet. God only knows what Charley could be doing to the house but as long as Kelly was safe I didn't care. We left our phones off all day and ordered room service twice. It was strangely nice given the circumstances. But as we went to sleep that night Kelly suggested that she should head back tomorrow alone to smooth things over if Charley was there. I didn't like the idea but she was right. She could talk sense into her, I had a feeling every time Charley saw me now she would explode.

We didn't sleep that much that night, I was worried but also knew that no way Charley would harm Kelly so I finally made peace with our plan and drifted off to sleep. I woke up at 8 in the morning because Kelly was shaking me;

"Wake up."

"I'm awake, I'm awake, what is it?"

"Charley has texted me. She wants to see me and only me at 9 this morning at our house."

"Okay, well that's, erm, that's good is it? Was that our plan anyway?"

"Yeah, I was going to head home and hope she was going to be there and now I know she definitely will be."

"Do you want me to come?"

"No, best not. We need this to go nice and smooth."

"Okay but shall I come and wait in the car around the corner at least?"

"Listen, it will be fine. She is my sister, she won't hurt me so don't worry. Go and use the pool and get some breakfast. I'll call you as soon as it's sorted and you can come home."

"If we still have one!"

"Behave." She gave me a kiss and left. I text her to say she was taking the car so she would have to come back for me. Checkout was at 12 so we agreed to meet then downstairs then. I spent the next few hours in a state. I wanted to text or call her to see how it was going but didn't want to disturb any progress. She did text about 9.30 to say all was okay and she'd see me at 12.

I called Rocket and Ethan and filled them in on my USA daytime soap drama-styled week and they asked if there was anything they could do but I told them it was under control and thanked them before hanging up in case Kelly was calling. I ventured down to the lobby just before 12 and checked out then waited outside for her. It got to 12.15 and she still hadn't shown up. I tried calling but it went straight to voicemail. I was shitting myself. What now? Can I phone the police? What would they do? A grown woman went to meet her sister at 9 in the morning and isn't back by midday, so what? *Quick call the FBI.*

It was about half past, I was about to book a taxi and just head back when Kelly called;

"You okay?" I asked even before the phone was to my ear.

"Hi, yeah sorry, all good. Sorry I'm not back there to get you but Charley wants to spend the day together."

"I guess that is understandable. Is she, you know, sort of normal again?"

"Yeah she has calmed down and feeling a bit remorseful."

"Okay that's good. I'll head home then."

"Actually, we want to spend the day together here, you know, sorting mum's stuff together. You don't mind do you?"

"No of course not, I'll make myself busy for the day. What time shall I head back?"

She said something to Charley that I couldn't make out nor the reply. "Okay to hang on until about 8pm? We want to have dinner and just spend time together."

"Yeah no problem," fucking 8pm! What the hell was I going to do for eight hours? "I'll see if the boys are about and maybe have a pint or two. You sure you're okay though?"

"Absolutely fine. Thanks for understanding. Love you. See you at 8!"

"See you at 8, love you too."

And the phone went dead.

I managed to drag the longest day ever out. It's hard to kill time on a Monday when you have a big cloud looming over you, in this instance, metaphorical and actual, it was a shit day considering it was the so-called summer. I went to see Rocket at work, I went to the cinema, I ate and then I met Ethan for a pint. It finally rolled around to about 7.45pm so I booked a cab and said goodbye to Ethan and said we'd catch up on Friday.

The cab got me home just before 8 but thought I'd risk it. I took a deep breath at the front door, pleased to see that I still had a door, and stepped in, bracing myself for whatever was thrown my way. Turns out, nothing.

"Hello!?" I shouted a few times without response. I looked around the house and it was definitely empty. No note either. I wondered if maybe they had gone to the hospital and decided that was probably it. I took my phone out to call Kelly when it started ringing. Just a number, no name.

I answered it and slowly put it to me ear, "Hello?"

"Hello, *bro,*" it was Charley.

"Charley? Is that you? Why you on a different number?"

"Shut the fuck up! Now listen to what I'm going to say."

"What are yo....."

"Is that shutting the fuck up?! I mean it." She waited as I didn't say anything, "good boy. Now I'm going to give you an address in a minute, memorise it and then head to it."

"What? Are you and Kelly in trouble? Where are you?"

"Kelly is in trouble yes."

"WHAT do you mean? Where is she?"

"Oh, she is right here with me. But she is far from safe."

"Charley, what are you going on about? Put Kelly on."

"As you wish." She put the phone to what I assume was Kelly's gagged mouth as all I got was a muffled attempted scream of *Haarrrrry.*"

"KELLY?! KELLY?!"

"You see *bro*, she is far from alright."

"I swear to God Charley, you fucking lunatic, if you have hurt one hair on her body I will actually kill you!"

"Like you did my mother you mean?!"

"I didn't! Where are you? I'm coming to get her right now!"

"Slow down there Romeo. All in good time. Firstly though I'll need you to get a pen a paper and write this down."

"What? Why?"

"If you want to see her again I suggest you do as I ask."

I did what she said and found the paper. "Okay, got some, what's the address?"

"This isn't for the address.... It's for your confession."

"What confession?"

"The one where you admit killing my mum."

"For fucksake Charley. I didn't kill her, who do you think I am?!"

"If you want to see Kelly again you will write down, I KILLED IRIS and sign it, simple as that."

"Is this a joke? Are you two pissed and winding me up? Put Kelly on."

"DO IT!!" She yelled the loudest I'd ever heard anyone yell, and then my phone beeped, it was a picture message and it showed Kelly tied up and covered in blood and tears.

"Charley, what the fuck have you done? WHERE ARE YOU? TELL ME NOW!"

"OOH aren't you the macho man? Write it down and stick it to the fridge."

"If I do that will you tell me where to find her?"

"Cross my heart and hope to die." I could even imagine her doing it.

I scribbled down what she wanted and stuck it to the fridge. "It's done, now where are you?

She gave me an address and I knew where it was. I raced to my taxi, not worrying about the two pints I had earlier and raced to the old industrial estate, which was the address I was given. I'd decided I was just going to walk in and punch Charley as hard as possible, even if this was some sort of elaborate hoax. She told me no police that made me think it is probably a wind up, but it was a bit extreme to say the least.

So I didn't know quite what was going on but I knew I had to get to the warehouse as quickly as possible. Kelly was in danger, she might not have believed that her sister was this dangerous and unstable but I certainly did. I didn't have time to think what I could be walking into.

I was in my taxi and heading to the address Charley had given me. It was about fifteen minutes away but I was going to do it in ten. For all I knew, it could be crucial minutes. I made sure I didn't break the law by going through any red lights or driving like a movie car chase but I did use the roads that didn't have cameras on them so I could hurry. I had to head south towards Hayes common, luckily I knew the old industrial park that they were at, it had been empty for years, how Charley knew about it I wasn't sure.

I made it there in nine minutes and the first thing I saw was Kelly's BMW. The passenger door was open and the lights were on, but the engine wasn't. I crept up to it, I'm not sure why, I was pretty sure nobody was in it. I got there and checked inside to see Kelly's bag but no sign of her or Charley. There was just the usual stuff in her bag, she always kept a tidy bag, and I checked through and didn't notice anything out of the ordinary except her passport was next to her bag, along with Charley's. I grabbed them both and put them in my pocket. I wasn't sure what why or what Charley was planning. Surely she didn't know about our money coming through. Kelly had promised not to say anything yet as I had suggested that Charley could flip given recent events. Looks like I might have been right.

I made my way to the door of the unit I was told to head to, it was closed so I opened it and as quietly as possible stepped through. It was dark as soon as I closed the door behind me, I suppose it blocked out the car lights. It wasn't pitch black though as there were some dim lights up ahead, I headed towards them. I thought I heard some music as I was getting closer, old fashioned music, Vera Lynn maybe? That wasn't important but as I approached the room with the lights shining, it was one of those decorator lights like one I had in my shed. Once I was next to that I looked around and saw Kelly. She was tied to a chair, she looked gagged but her head was slumped forward with her hair falling downwards so I couldn't be sure but my stomach lurched. I ran towards her praying she was still alive.

The short distance I covered in a second or two and slid on my legs to get to her quicker. I got up on my knees quickly and lifted her head.

"Kelly? Kelly? Can you hear me?!" I wasn't shouting but the panic through my voice meant it was coming out loudly. "Kelly!" I took her face in my hands. She had bloody above her eye and coming out of her nose as well as a split lip. She looked a mess but she was breathing, thank God. I removed the gag.

"Harrrrry?" Was the slow whisper back.

"It's me baby, it's me. What's happened? Can you get up?" I was throwing questions at her without needing answers.

"Where, where am I?"

"It doesn't matter honey, let's get you out of here."

"Charley? Where is she?" She was still struggling to get her words out and I'd pretty much stopped waiting and was trying to undo her wrists from the cable ties. Why the fuck didn't I bring a knife or something.

"I don't know, but listen. I'm going to have to find something to cut this ties, I can't do it with my fingers."

"No. don't leave me... Please."

"I'm not going far; I just need to find something sharp."

"Do you want to borrow this?" I span round and saw Charley. She was stood about ten yards away, dressed black trousers and a black hoodie; she even had black shoes and black gloves on. That isn't what I noticed first though. She was holding my biggest kitchen knife.

Kelly screamed.

"Charley. What the fuck are you doing? This is your sister!"

Charley casually strolled around the room without taking her stare off me. "She's no sister of mine."

157

"You're not thinking Charley, of course she is, and your best friend. I saw the effort you put into our wedding. I even saw the book you made planning it all."

"Ha-ha, yeah mum said you had been snooping, I knew you would. That's why I created and planted that book. I hated the whole thing. You, her, the day. And as for being my best friend and sister? That is *so* sweet you say that," she mocked, "but no sister or *friend* of mine would hide ten million pounds from me!"

"Jesus Christ." I said, realising just how crazy this woman was, "Does money really mean that much to you?! This is your SISTER!"

"Wrong. She *was* my sister. Now she's nothing. Well, not nothing, she is still very important to me." She paused for a second or two as I waited, "everything in her will goes to me. Everything in your will goes to her. You see where this is going right?"

"Charley, you're wrong. You can let us go. The money isn't left to you." I let that hang as she seemed to think about it. "Come on Charley, this isn't you. You want the money? You can have it! I don't care about it, but I care about Kelly. And I know you do too."

She looked at me, in fact, through me. Her eyes looked like they had nothing behind them. Like a great white shark, they were empty. I carried on trying, "You couldn't kill her. I know you like to think you could but there is no way you could and you know it."

"Why couldn't I." She almost smirked, "I've already killed our mum."

THIRTY FIVE

As the words flowed through my brain the first thing I heard was Kelly whimpering. I finally tried to stand up but I wasn't sure my legs were going to work. I wobbled but made it to my feet.

"You're wrong Charley. I know you might feel guilty about it for not being there when she died but you didn't kill her." I was talking louder as Kelly's crying was getting louder.

"Don't try and play the high and mighty with me you tosser. I know I killed her."

"She died of old age, she was very ill. You'll see there was nothing you could do about it."

"You idiot," she let out another laugh, "I know I killed her because I poisoned her."

I was stunned into silence. Kelly was still sobbing; I think Charley may have told her this as it didn't appear to be news to her. But I also seemed to sense a feeling of defeat in her. I honed in on the faint music in the background, it was Vera Lynn, *We'll Meet Again*. It was on repeat.

"What... What do you mean? Poisoned her?"

"Well, brainbox, I'd been poisoning her for weeks." She noticed that I had noticed the music. "This was her favourite song by the way." Thought it would be rather relevant."

"I don't understand," I finally said after about a minute, still not quite accepting what I had been told, "But she wasn't poisoned. You'll see when the autopsy report comes back in."

"It already did you moron! The police will be here within the next ten minutes I'd imagine."

"Why the hell would the police be coming? I told you I wouldn't call them and I didn't, I swear."

"I knew *you* wouldn't, you're too much of a wuss. No no, I called them."

"What? Why the hell would you have called them?!"

She took a couple of steps closer to me. "You really are a silly man aren't you? I've called the police because I've just caught my mother's killer, and my sister's abductor and killer *and* my long term abuser."

My legs gave way a little as the words were hitting me. "You won't get away with this."

"Oh really? Why is that? All you have done is moan to the world and his wife about my mum. You've been left in charge of her medicine, you publicly belittle her and me all the time, and you make jokes about us dying. How about your wife? Let's say from an abusive relationship, found out and spoke to her sister about it and we planned to get away from you but you found out, caught us, killed her and tried to kill me but I fought back. Oh yes, I think all the motive is there for all to see,"

There were no words for what felt like an eternity. All I could hear was Kelly's sobs and the faint music.

"Well," I was trying to put on some false bravado to buy time until the police got here. If indeed they were actually coming. "How could you possibly think this was going to work? There's a lot of difference between moaning about your in-laws to becoming a murderer don't you think? You're not the brightest are you!?" I wasn't sure if insulting her was the best idea but I was hoping to anger her into a mistake. It didn't work.

She was getting closer to me and started talking in a theatrical way; "*All the world's a stage; And all the men and women merely players; They have their exits and entrances, And one man in his time plays many parts.*" All I could do was look back at her. I should have been looking for a way out of this for me and Kelly but my brain, nor legs, seemed to be working.

"Hey! Brainbox?!" Charley was clicking her gloved fingers in my face now. "As You Like It. Act II Scene VII." I just continued to look at her simply not knowing what to say or do. "It's Shakespeare. I'm sure you knew that though hey?"

I didn't.

"But you didn't even know who he was?!" It was the best I could find.

"Do you want to know the hardest thing about this whole plan? It was having to listen to your condescending bullshit for a year. *Pretending* I was stupid! Playing up to it to make you feel like a big man. And you fell right into my trap didn't you?"

This was crazy. But she was right. I'd been played like a fiddle. "But what about Kelly? She must have noticed you'd suddenly become dumb over night?"

"Do me a favour. *She's* the dumb one. She doesn't know what day it is unless she is told."

I simply didn't know what to say *or* do, I checked Kelly and she was just crying, maybe in a state of shock. I crouched down and cuddled her as much as I could, I tried pulling on her restraints but they would not be moved.

"Ah, *The course of true love never did run smooth.* That one is A Midsummer Night's Dream." Charley was saying it crouching down in front of us both.

"So you're actually a Shakespeare expert are you?!"

"Not really. Never a big fan. No, science. Science is my area of expertise."

"Science?" An hour ago I wouldn't have thought she could spell it. "I suppose this is where you got your idea of killing your own mother from."

"Thallium Sulphate."

"Thallium Sulphate? What's that then?"

"It's what I used, sorry; it's what *you* used to kill her."

"Well I don't even know what it is never mind where to find it."

"It's under your sink."

I had no idea what she was going on about. She must have planted something but surely the police could trace poison from where and when it's bought these days? "I think you're clutching here. There is no *Thallium Sulphate* under my sink."

"Rat poison."

My heart sank and my stomach felt like it was going to fall out of my arse. "What?"

"Rat poison. The rat poison *you* bought online with your card. Oh hang on, it was me that bought it with your card wasn't it? Oh dear."

"But... but surely that isn't possible to buy anymore. There has to be safeguards about it."

"Silly boy, I bought the real, low grade rat poison online with your card, then, before I gave you it back I visited another site I knew about. The dark web is a magical place. The rat poison I acquired is illegal in this country; in fact, I think even vermin-killers in other countries need a licence to carry this stuff. But also, I wasn't sure it would quite do the trick so I added some soluble Thallium salt to it, so it was quicker for mum. Now, *unfortunately*, there might be a small way of tracing this particular purchase back to you. And as luck would have it, they've obviously picked up the poison in the tox-screen of the autopsy. To put it bluntly, *bro*, you're fucked."

All I could think about was that bloody Dolly Parton film when they poison their boss. I needed to think and think fast. "But your poor mum, she didn't deserve this." I was going for the heart-strings. It wasn't going to work, probably because she didn't have a heart.

She laughed. "You're actually getting dumber by the minute. My mum *knew* about this! She was miserable, in pain, dying very slowly and she thought instead of running the risk of me doing it illegally and getting caught, we hatched this plan. She never liked you did she? And the money you tried hiding from us, just made us more determined. I can live with it because in my eyes, it was basically euthanasia."

This was incredible. I would have sworn that Charley would have thought euthanasia was something to do with kids in India and China but here I was, completely at this woman's mercy. "What about the pain it must have caused Iris at the end. Do you not care about that?"

"It's a good point that. Thallium is actually odourless and tasteless so she didn't even know she was getting it. Well, I say that. She did, obviously. But what I should say is that you didn't know you were giving it to her."

"What?"

"Every time you made her a cup of tea in that final week I'd pop in and slip some in there. It doesn't take long to get enough into their system. And she drank a lot of tea. But if you ever bothered to notice, she only drank it when you were there to make it."

"Why?"

"Why? Well we had to figure out when it was best to give it to her. It couldn't be in food because we all ate the same stuff most of the time and we also wanted to make sure that if there was some magical way of tracing the time of ingestion, it would fit in with you always being there."

"I just can't believe it."

"Well you had better. We have covered all bases. Thallium was actually a stroke of genius. It would only take between one and two grams of it. The tea you made her for that week all had poison in them. It's all it took. Much more believable for a dim cabbie to use to poison his mother-in-law like this. My original plan was Suxamethonium."

I'd stopped listening as I'd spotted a large piece of wood not too far away from me, out of Charley's eye-line but could I get to it? I asked; "Suxa-what?"

"It's an extremely lethal poison, but still obtainable from the right places. But it wouldn't be believable that someone like *you* would know what it is."

"Oh hang on," I stood up and slowly started edging my way left, "Isn't that the poison used on the Russian spy in London?" It was working; she hadn't noticed my slight movement as she was wrapped up in impressing me with her plan.

"Alexander Litvinenko? Yes, well, a version of it."

"That wouldn't have been a nice way for Iris to go would it?" I was getting closer to the piece of wood; Kelly spotted me just as Charley put the gag back around her mouth and stood up properly. Kelly's eyes were wide, I just hope she didn't give me away by accident; she was in a real state. Charley was looking at her. In sympathy or in victory I wasn't sure.

"True. *Malignant hyperthermia,* not pleasant. The skeletal muscle oxidative metabolism increases uncontrollably. That overwhelms the body's ability to supply oxygen and remove carbon dioxide. *Obviously* leading to circulatory collapse." She turned to face me.

"Obviously." I said as I swung the big piece of wood as hard as I could and cracking it around Charley's head. The wood wasn't that strong and splintered in half. She hit the floor quickly but was not knocked out, and she still had hold of the knife. I jumped on her and made a grab for her wrist, we tussled momentarily but I was a lot stronger and managed to smack her wrist a couple of times on the hard ground making her release the knife, she manged to knee me between the legs, she didn't get much power but it hit the spot and I lost balance and toppled off her but towards the knife. I managed to grab it as we both staggered to our feet. Charley picked up a bit of the splintered wood and ran behind Kelly holding the jaggered edge to her throat.

"Lose the knife!" She yelled at me.

I couldn't risk her hurting Kelly. "Charley, please, don't do this!" The fight was starting to fall away from me and I could feel the tears start to form. Not that I'd ever thought I'd be in a position like this, but when you watch the movies you scream at them to attack the bad guy or out smart or out fight them but this was reality, my body was shaking, I felt I couldn't clench a fist anymore. Some sort of fight or flight response I guess. All I wanted now was to get out of here with Kelly and I was going to have to plead. Either that or I wanted to wake up in bed with her right now and this was just a bad dream. The tears started to come and were blurring my vision. "Charley, please, let's sort this out. Just let her go. Kill me but please, let her go. Have the money, I really don't care but please, just don't hurt her anymore."

"Drop. The. Knife!" There wasn't an ounce of emotion in this woman in front of me. So I had to do what she said and I dropped it down in front of myself.

"Kick it over here!"

I kicked it but to the right of her and she was holding the wood in her right hand. She looked down at it then back at me.

"I think this maybe where we say our goodbyes. Kelly first?" Charley said dropping the wood and bending down for the knife, as she came back up with it there was a shout from the door;

"POLICE! POLICE! EVERYBODY STAY WHERE THEY ARE!" There were police officers heading into the building. I didn't look to see where they were but fortunately Charley did, I launched myself forward punching her as hard as I could above where Kelly was sat, and catching her perfectly on the temple, I put so much into it and was in mid-air when I connected and ended up falling down on top of her, the knife slicing through my left shoulder. The pain was immense but it didn't matter, Charley was out cold. I rolled onto my back and saw the police offices, looked like they were in riot gear, closing in on us. It was all upside down and I was exhausted. I almost sobbed with sheer relief.

But...

I had forgotten that the police were actually here to arrest *me* off the back of whatever lies Charley had fed them and they were on me in no time, rolling my onto my front and cuffing me, the pain from my shoulder was like having a hot poker pressed on me.

"Wait, wait!" I was protesting, "its not me you want, it her!" I was getting pulled up to my feet by two of the biggest blokes I'd ever seen and I was nodding down to the motionless Charley.

"I don't think so do you?" The almost seven feet, heavily attired bobby said to me. "You're nicked sunshine." He sounded like a T.V copper who lived for saying that as he slapped handcuffs tightly onto me.

"Ask her, ask Kelly. She'll tell you everything!" I protested with my voice going higher and higher.

163

Charley was starting to make a strange groan as she started to come back around. Another officer was taking off Kelly's restraints and removing her gag. She was coughing, maybe even choking on her many tears.

"Ma'am? Are you okay? Can you stand?" The officer was helping Kelly to her feet. Another two were starting to get Charley up too. Asking her the same, no sign of cuffs for her.

"Kelly! Are you okay?!" I was desperate to go and give her a hug, hold her in my arms for at least a week. "Tell them what's happened."

Kelly rubbed her forehead and wiped away the blood from her face as best she could. The police officer asked her what had happened here.

She looked at Charley and then all around to take in the surroundings then at me, and started shaking.

"It was *him!*" Kelly slowly raised her arm and pointed straight at me. "He brought me here and tied me up. He told me he murdered my mother, and that he was going to kill me and my sister!" It came out in a horrid shrill and shaking sobs.

What was happening?! "Kelly? What, what are you doing!?"

"He's been threatening it since I moved in with him. I had to marry him, he told me he would kill my mum if I didn't," the tears were flowing in an epic surge again, "but he killed her anyway!" She turned and buried her head into the policeman and let out a wail.

"It's true." I turned to see Charley now talking, "It's why I called you guys. He brought Kelly here but I followed and called you. But I thought I could get Kelly free, we planned to escape to the airport and get away from him forever but he caught us and stopped us, he had a knife!" She started to sob too. "And then he took our passports. We were caught and knew we were in big trouble. Thank God you arrived when you did. He was about to cut Kelly's throat when I just launched myself at him, even though he managed to get the better of me I like to think it gave us just enough time for you to arrive."

This can't be right, I must have an explanation for all this but nothing was coming out. All I could muster was a feeble; "Kelly?"

"Two passports here Sarg..." The policeman had taken them out of my back pocket.

"Kelly?" It was again the only thing I could summon, in a weak pathetic way.

She slowly pulled her head away from the officer and looked at me, through all the blood and tears she just screamed; "rot in hell you monster!"

THIRTY SIX

It was three years later I next saw Kelly. I was in my new surroundings of HM Wakefield. It was a category A prison that housed the worst of the worst in the country. I thought it was a bit harsh that I get sentenced and sent here, but apparently murdering pensioners and attempting the murder of your wife puts you in that bracket. At least I said I always wanted to visit Yorkshire.

I got the call that I had a visitor, rare in itself. Ethan and Rocket did visit when they could, they knew I hadn't done any of this and were trying to help with my appeals but as I was told by many, I was wasting my time. It was a slam dunk case.

I still couldn't get my head around it. I'd had three years so far to try and still had another twenty-six to go. Was this all for money? Kelly not only would have had it anyway but I was sure she didn't even know about it when she met me. I had resided myself to the realisation I would never know until my visit this day.

I had sworn to myself I would never speak to her, or Charley if I ever had the chance. I didn't think I would even see them again. Kelly didn't even come to the court for the trial and did it via a video link, adding to the effect I suppose. Charley had and won the jury over with her performance. My lawyer said our goose was cooked from that moment on.

I was taken to the visitation room. It was just like the movies, a thick sheet of soundproofed glass with a phone on either side to talk to each other. I was lead to my seat and slowly sat down. I wasn't sure whether to even bother picking up the receiver but after a moment or two and a couple of deep breaths I picked it up.

"Hi." Kelly said as I put my ear to the phone.

"Hi." I gave back, unbelievably still taken in by her beauty. She actually looked better than I remembered. But I suppose having ten million quid at your disposal does that.

"I just thought I'd come and see how you are coping."

"Awfully kind of you." I always did sarcasm well. "Why wouldn't I be coping? It's lovely in here. How is St Tropez?"

"Haven't been."

"Good."

"Yet."

"What do you want Kelly?"

"I just wanted to see how you were doing, honestly."

"Rub it in you mean?"

"No. Not at all. I just wanted you to know it wasn't personal. I really didn't dislike you. It was a fun year."

"Are you actually mental? Not personal? Do you even understand what that means? This was as personal as it gets!"

I don't think it bothered her one bit.

"Well, I just didn't want you to think I didn't enjoy any of it."

"OH Kelly? That's *so* lovely to hear, thank you. Now kindly, Fuck off! Thanks."

"I thought maybe you'd want some answers?"

Of course I did. I had a hundred questions. But I didn't want to give her the satisfaction of maybe burying some of her own demons. "Nope." And I went to get up.

"It was planned from the start!" She got in quickly before I put the phone back. Okay, she had me.

"What do you mean?"

"From the start. You were our play from the start."

"Start of what? Us?"

"Yeah." To be fair she looked sheepish. Fucking right too.

"The broken down car?"

She looked at me, not even blinking, there looked to be some sadness in her eyes but who knew with this witch.

"Before actually. Charley was working in a bar and over-heard James, your solicitor, talking about you and your expensive bit of a land and we hatched a plan. Drunk plan at first but we realised it could work. It would take care of our mum, and then us financially for life."

"James?"

"Yeah. It's why I had to make sure he didn't make our wedding or I'd never go with you to your meetings with him. He'd have recognised me." She saw the drop of my eyes. "Oh, honey, you thought I just *trusted* you to go to the meetings on your own and add me to your will and estate? That's so sweet. And of course I did. Because you did it."

She was right, I had. Despite James telling me not to. "But how did it all start? How did you get information out of him?"

"As I said, he was in the bar sat talking on his phone to somebody. His wife I think. Charley over-heard snippets of conversation and soon got the gist. He came in quite regularly so that night after work we started planning. We'd get the information from him, details of this *client*, you, and get into your life and get married, divorce you and take half the money."

"I'd have taken that deal."

"I know, but mum came up with this new plan. We thought four million split down the middle after a divorce and solicitor fees and all that wouldn't actually be enough. Even when it got to a higher amount we still thought we'd take the whole lot. And put mum out of her misery without getting ourselves into trouble. You have to admit, it was the perfect plan."

"It was, is in fact. Just a shame it cost two lives. Mine and your mum's."

"Sometimes we need to lose small battles in order to win the war." She quoted to me. "So, as I was saying, the next time James came in we started on him. I would be at the bar and Charley working. Seducing, I suppose you could say. It's amazing how happily married men fall quickly for women that show even the slightest bit of attention."

"Would it surprise me? I mean, I was one of them wasn't I?!"

She laughed. "Yes, I suppose you were. Sorry about that. So after a couple of months getting this information slowly and subtly out of him, we knew you were the target and the operation was a go."

I was going to kill James. "But how did you get the information so easily from him. He's better than that."

"Wrong, I mean, he should be. But at the end of the day, a man is a man. All susceptible to the charms of an attractive, forward lady."

I could do nothing but slowly shake my head whilst attempting to consume all the information. "Bloody Charley. Or should I say *the black widow*? She is deadly. Is there nothing she wouldn't have done for this *plan* of yours?"

Kelly just looked back at me and smiled. "Not Charley I'm afraid. James was all me."

The words shook me like an earthquake. My vision quickly blurred and my head spun. My stomach movement like when water disappears quickly from an aeroplane toilet once you've flushed. I wobbled and put my hand on the desk in front of me to steady myself "But..."

"But?"

"You and him? He's in his fifties!"

"I didn't say I enjoyed it but it was integral to our plans. You could say I took one… in fact, I took several, for the team."

"You're disgusting."

She just scoffed, "I didn't see you complaining when I was doing it with you."

"I thought we were in love!"

"Oh baby… I think *you* were."

I didn't have a response to that. I just sat there with my hand rubbing my face and hair trying to digest it all. She carried on;

"He also set up the account so it could be accessed by just me. Not needing you or your signature. Little did you know," she didn't stop there, "and of course, getting into character was easy with him; I just wore this and became Rachel." She pulled out a black wig. Strange the things you can bring into a prison without query.

"Is this supposed to impress me? Make me feel better? Or worse?!"

"None of those. I just thought you might recognise it?"

I didn't know what she meant. I remembered seeing a wig in Charley's room that time but so what? Even if it's the same wig Kelly was holding now what did it matter? I just shrugged my shoulders and shook my head.

"What about with these?" Kelly said pulling out a big pair of sunglasses.

I still didn't get what she was getting at. "What? I don't get it. You like going out dressed as Jackie Onassis?"

"Charley also wore this wig. In fact she wore this wig, with these sunglasses the first time you met her."

"She was blonde when I met her! At my house that time when she was sat on my table."

"*Can you get me to Swallow in five minutes?* Ring any bells?"

Not for the first time a tonne of bricks hit me. "The woman that got in my cab."

"That's the one. How else could we make sure we got you to be my shining knight?"

I couldn't believe that that was Charley. I suppose you don't pay too much attention to some customers, especially in the back when all you can occasionally see looking back at you is a big dark pair of glasses. "Very clever, well done."

"Thank you. And the rest, as they say, is history."

"But why were they both so horrible to me? I mean, most blokes wouldn't have put up with what I did and just thrown them and probably you, out."

Through what I considered her legitimate smile she responded, "we had to run the risk. We needed you to hate them and let everyone you know hate them. In fact, even people you didn't know. How many of your customers did you moan about them to? Even new customers I bet." She of course, was absolutely spot on. I listened more as she continued, "We thought about calming it down just in case you really did have enough but every time you wanted to I just used my magic touch. Men are so easy. You would have done anything for me."

She was right. "But, I still don't know why so extreme? I mean, you would have had the money anyway. In fact, you would have had more because you have to split this with Charley, whereas I'd have just let you do what you want with it if we carried on our lives together."

I think I'd hit a nerve, she looked a bit shaken for the first time, almost as if she hadn't thought about that fact.

"Family is more important." It was a wobbly reply, and kind of feeble.

"Family? You killed your mother."

"At her request." The answer was back quickly, she seemed rattled that's for sure.

"Maybe. But that money could have got her the best treatment. Maybe kept her around for another ten years."

She took her time and a couple of breaths and with that she seemed back in control. "She didn't want ten more years. And she wanted her girls to be sorted for life. She was right. It worked. Who knows, maybe we'll for another gullible fool with lots of money. We seem to be pretty good at it. By the way, Charley asked how the showers are and did you get the soap on a rope she sent you?"

I didn't bother acknowledging the comment. "You won't get away with this you know?"

"Oh honey," she started to put her stuff back in her bag, "I already have."

"These conversations are recorded!"

"Nice try."

"I'm coming for you, mark my words! I'll fucking get you!" I punched the glass. I heard the guards open the door and start heading my way. "I've got nothing else to do! I'll make it the upmost important thing in my life to get you!"

She just looked at me and smiled before speaking into the phone one last time and saying; "It's *utmost.*"

The END

Printed in Great Britain
by Amazon

44873617R00104